WANTING MOORE

MARY VINE

WANTING MOORE

Published by Windtree Press in cooperation with Melland Publishing, LLC.

Windtree Press

Portland, Oregon

https://windtreepress.com

Melland Publishing, LLC

Caldwell, ID

http://mellandpublishing.com

Cover Design by Ed Parker, Jr.

Published in the United States of America

Publishing History

1st Edition 2011, Black Lyon Publishing

2nd Edition 2019, Windtree Press

Wanting Moore / Mary Vine – 2nd edition

Print ISBN 978-1-950387-35-9

Epub ISBN 978-1-950387-36-6

CHAPTER 1

August, 1866

Isabella Moore sat shoulder to shoulder in a stagecoach of bodies, packed like a can of sardines. Besides the self-serving attitude of the driver, Micah, all of the occupants of the vehicle treated the only woman with respect. All eyes turned to her, but as the only girl in a family of seven children, she was used to being singled out. Still, she wore a simple gray dress and a bonnet that covered much of her face, hoping to pass as an old maid, which in reality she was.

Isabella's obsession with the idea of finding a gold nugget, combined with her dream of teaching children brought her here. Or, at least to this point in her travel from Prairie City to Haines, Oregon, by way of the Cracker City-Haines Stage Road.

Thankfully, she sat next to the door and had only to feel the body of the man at one side. It didn't take her long to decide to keep words at a minimum, as she continued to be under constant perusal from the bonnet on her head to the shoes on her feet. The seat allowed her the opportunity to gaze out the window beside her, which also helped a great deal.

The smell of man assailed her nostrils, from tobacco to unclean bodies. If that were not enough to gag her, the rolling of the stage gave her motion sickness. She'd been served the same thing for breakfast and lunch – bacon, beans and flapjacks - and contemplated seeing it all again at her feet when the stage came to an abrupt stop.

Her head barely missed a stream of chewing tobacco aimed out a crack in the door as she looked to see what the problem was.

A kerchief covered the lower portion of a man's face and the sun reflected off the barrel of his pistol. The best she could see, there were two men.

Isabella was well-read enough to know that the usual stagecoach robber didn't want to kill the passengers as much as make a killing on a roll of bills or gold found in the area. Still, from the groans and sighs of those around her, she knew she wasn't alone in wondering what would happen to them after being left with nothing but the clothes on their backs. It took every ounce of strength she possessed to remain calm and focused.

In mere moments, one armed crook had the occupants lined up against a fallen log, while the other placed valuables in a nap sack.

The man with the gun sat her across from the others on a log by herself, now facing his back. Isabella knew he did this because a lady of repute was rare in these parts and therefore valued.

"This will be all through in a minute, Miss, and you can go safely on your way."

She held her smile in, thinking his respect would get him into trouble this time. Thanks to her brothers, she'd already learned how to live in a world full of males and she'd used the advantage of being the only female child many times. Frankly, she really didn't like being treated like a helpless fool. Studying the scene closely, she waited for an opportune time to make her move.

Isabella supposed she could have used the gun tucked into her garter but decided someone could get hurt in the crossfire.

Instead, she tried to emulate the picture of innocent distress, with her hand clutching the bodice of her dress, her eyes now focused away from the masked man as if she couldn't bear to look at him.

She gave herself a mental pat on the back for putting most of her money in her shoe. In a moment of convenience, Isabella took that same shoe and planted it squarely on the back of the gunman in front of her and he fell flat on his masked face.

Before he could recover from the shock, two passengers in the line knocked over the other crook, while still others lashed onto the man on the ground as he wiped tiny pebbles from his forehead.

The whole canyon filled with the sound of hoots, hollers and slaps on the back. Many hats came off in her honor and she curtsied demurely. Once everyone's valuables were accounted for, the two men, with ropes around their wrists, joined passengers on top of the stage.

After this moment of reprieve, Isabella was helped back into the stage carefully, as if made of porcelain, and did not just save the day. She wondered if they were like her brothers, not wanting to face that a mere slip of a girl could outdo them.

On they bumped and rolled up a mountain. She knew this would be a difficult trek but wasn't prepared for the steep, narrow, hand-hewn road.

Those in the coach all leaned to the left so that the weight of the wagon wasn't perched too close to a dangerous precipice. She imagined how frightening it'd be to sit on the top of the stage, clinging on for dear life.

The mules treaded slowly and then the stage came to a complete stop. All passengers were ordered to get out and walk over the tip of the mountain peak.

Once the driver made it as far as he could on mule team power, many helped him anchor the wagon to drill steels imbedded into rock. This kept the coach from crashing back down the area they'd just traveled.

Confident she'd made it through the roughest part, she boarded the stage with a smile. The rest of the journey would be a picnic compared to what they'd been through so far. Between horrendous bumps, Isabella listened to the golden dreams of the men traveling with her.

Isabella's jovialness departed when she heard Micah yell at the mules to move faster. *Move faster?* They were going downhill.

The riders squared their shoulders and aligned their feet for balance. One man gripped a rosary and made the sign of the cross.

"This is usual," sounded a voice beside her. "The driver is in a hurry to get supplies and mail to those waiting, but don't worry. He's experienced."

"He won't get any money if he kills himself," she couldn't help but add.

"It's a rough job, but he can do it," said another voice.

She nodded, then closed her eyes, silently praying for help. Voices raised in panic interrupted her prayer. She opened her eyes in time to see the stage roll off the road. Instantly, the beating of her heart drowned out any other noise.

When Isabella regained consciousness, she lay outside the stage. As she spit dirt from her mouth, she felt a split lip and her knee stung, reminding her of what a childhood skinned knee felt like. Worst of all, her lower leg throbbed with a pain she had never experienced before.

Her wounds told her she fell in a distorted way, no doubt because of the way they were all situated together and then suddenly separated.

Others had injuries but not enough to keep most of them down. Two bodies lay unconscious; she tried to pull herself to the one nearest her, but her injured leg wouldn't allow movement. Yet, it didn't matter as better-able men walked to them.

"These two are dead. The woman is moving around."

"Let's right the wagon," said Micah. "I think we can move on if we can pull the stage without one mule. Let's get going."

Isabella focused on the mule. He tried to stand, but couldn't, and the other mules stood awkwardly, pulled toward him. Two men went over to take the harness off and then Micah aimed his gun and shot the injured mule.

After pity, anger welled up from within and she blurted out, "Two people are dead here, can you not spare a little time to bury them?"

"Not trying to be disrespectful, ma'am, but I must get my load in. Cracker City is not far up the road. I'll send someone back for them."

Micah turned toward the men who'd righted the wagon, leaving a gaping hole where the door had been, and a tire with broken pegs. After he barked out a few more orders, men set to work repairing the wheel.

"Can you move, ma'am?" Micah asked.

The pain was excruciating. Isabella momentarily wondered if someone could carry her to the stage but cast the thought aside as she knew she wouldn't be riding comfortably. "It's unbearable to move."

"Can anybody stay back and wait with the woman until help arrives?"

Some men looked down, others looked away. How ironic it was, she thought, that she'd saved their valuables a few miles back and now the only one who wanted to help her was the crook.

"I think she'd do better with the wolves and cougars than with the likes of you, Kirkwood," said Micah.

Isabella only had enough energy to deal with the pain, let alone Micah who probably didn't care if she rotted here.

The crook said, "Is that the same foot you knocked me down with?"

She ignored him.

"Does my heart good," he said, holding up his bound hands. "I hear there's a Civil War butcher in Cracker City that can take care of that leg."

"Shut up, Kirkwood!" After a moment the voice added, "I'll stay with her."

Isabella looked from her swelling leg to see who had spoken. The man, or boy, looked younger than her, and had a firm, determined jaw. He reminded her of her younger brother, proud but naïve, and she didn't want anything to do with helping either of them become a man. She also didn't want to be responsible for keeping him from where he needed to be.

In a blink of an eye, Isabella had a gun in her hand. With teeth clenched in pain, she said to Micah, "I understand it's not too far to Cracker City, especially with you in charge. I'm staying here; just make sure the doctor knows about me."

"Are you sure?"

"The ride's too bumpy for me. I can't move. You go on. I can protect myself. I'm probably a better shot than most of you standing here."

CHAPTER 2

The wagon rushed off, in a continued frenzy to get to town. If Isabella's brothers learned about her predicament they'd all ride out to hogtie and bring her back home. That couldn't happen.

Inch by inch, she scooted herself with her arm and shoulder to the trunk of a wide pine. With a cry of pain, she righted herself against the tree, and slowly stretched her legs out in front of her.

While Isabella battled her pain, she tried to tell herself how fortunate she was to be alive. From her perch, she could see the backs of the two bodies now rigid in the shape they'd fallen. It deeply saddened her to think these men, who'd boarded this God-forsaken stagecoach with her, were no longer in this world. They had dreams like she did, and loved ones who'd miss them. When her eyes stopped on the twisted body of the dead mule, she cried.

She'd started away from home so happy, positive, believing all could be hers for the taking. She didn't feel that way now, however, lying here afraid to close her eyes lest some animal choose her for supper. And she so wanted to close her eyes and sleep to forget the predicament she was in.

Forgetting for one moment about her leg, she moved slightly to straighten the skirt of her dress, and the pain overtook her again. Isabella noticed the hem of her lucky dress had ripped in her fall. Somehow the thought made her laugh, then cry.

It was not unheard of to break a leg and then lose it. She feared what Kirkwood the Crook had insinuated was true, that the doctor would need to take her leg off.

WHEN GABRIEL STONE made it to where the stagecoach tumbled, it was almost dark. A part of a soiled white rag hung from a limb to mark his destination. He'd been told others planned to bury the dead, but they weren't on the trail. He hoped the men didn't wait too long or the bodies would become victims of the wild, if they hadn't already.

Gabriel checked the two bodies nearest him. He'd seen many dead in the war, but the difference was these two had their teeth. He never could understand defiling the dead by pulling enough teeth to fill barrels, which were then sent to England to make artificial teeth.

Gabriel heard two had lost their lives, but he now feared three since he didn't see any movement from the third body. Moving closer he heard a groan. A female groan, if he was not mistaken. *A woman! What was Micah thinking leaving her out here like this?* No doubt, he thought about the extra money for getting the stage where it needed to be in plenty of time.

"I'm here to help," he said calmly, but loud enough for her to hear.

The woman lifted her head, tensed, and aimed the gun at his chest.

"I'm a doctor," he said, raising both his hands. "Micah sent me out here."

The woman had been holding her breath. When she let it out, she grimaced.

He was not such a fool that he'd step closer to the barrel of a gun. She took a moment to size him up, he did the same.

He couldn't believe his eyes; he'd stumbled upon a wildflower in the middle of the woods. If he could say one word to describe her it would be color. Her disheveled red hair framed a peaches and cream complexion. Her eyes were green, the color of emeralds. Yet, besides the color of her eyes and hair, she chose a gray pinstriped dress to wear. The dress didn't seem to match her somehow, like she'd dressed not to draw attention to herself. The bonnet, now fallen down around her neck, had a wide bill that no doubt covered part of her face. Good idea for a woman crossing these mountains, he supposed.

Gabriel shook his head as if to clear it, he wasn't here to find a flower in the barren landscape of his existence, but to help another human being.

"Help," she said weakly, then laid the gun beside her.

"I'm going to check your head for injury first," he said, speaking slowly as if to a frightened child. He supposed she was not far removed from a child anyway. Twenty, if a day.

"You've got a goose egg on your head, how is your neck?"

She moved her head in a circle. "Fine, I think."

"Good. Circle your shoulders."

"My shoulder is sore," she said and put a hand on it. "I think it broke my fall."

"It doesn't feel like it's been dislocated. You probably broke your fall with your leg, I'm thinking."

She winced and put a hand on her upper thigh.

"Your hips?" he asked, but did not touch them.

"I'm pretty sure they're bruised, but okay."

He nodded. "It's hard to miss the swelling in your leg. I need to check it."

"I know," she said forlornly, tears welling up in her eyes at any little movement.

"I'll be as careful as I can."

"Thank you."

"I can give you some whiskey or some laudanum for the pain," said Gabriel with a furrowed brow.

Isabella had taken laudanum only once before and couldn't remember much of anything when under the influence. Being out in nowhere with a man she didn't know, was not the best time to use laudanum. Yet, her preacher spoke often about the perils of alcohol, but what other choice did she have when she couldn't stand the pain? "I'll take a little whiskey, I guess."

"I was hoping you'd choose the whiskey. The laudanum will put you out and I need to be able to call you awake if I need to."

The doctor went back to his mules for a moment and returned with a flask. He helped her take a swig, but because of the angle of the flask, the gulp was bigger than she'd wanted. The strong liquid burned her throat and made her cough. She moved and then cried out in pain.

"I'm sorry you are in so much pain."

"That makes two of us. Ouch!"

"I'm trying to be careful."

With two hands he felt every inch of her ankle and foot, then stopped and stared at the shin of her lower leg.

Fear overwhelmed her. Kirkwood described him as a butcher, and she worried about having to have part of her leg amputated.

Isabella carefully took the flask from the doctor and took two more sips, taking in as much as she could handle this time.

After a cough and the gritting of her teeth, she asked, "So, how long have you been a doctor? Mr. uh … "

"Stone. Gabriel Stone. I went to medical school before the Civil War and then started practicing during the war. I don't need to practice anymore; I do the real thing now. Sometimes," he said with a frown.

"Sometimes?"

"These days I only help out in emergencies."

"So, your experience runs with cannon and gunshot wounds then, huh? Maybe you can't help me with my leg."

"If you want to call in another doctor, I think you are out of luck, ma'am. I'm at a disadvantage; I don't know your name."

"Isabella Moore. No, I understand that medical help is rare out here. It's just that you look baffled when you look at my leg, which makes me a little concerned." Horrified was more like it.

"I am baffled, to find a woman out here without supervision."

"Oh, that," she said with a wave of her hand. "I can take care of myself. I can shoot a gun - Ouch."

"Still, it's not right."

His words spiked her anger. "I'm injured, you know, and didn't want to have to babysit some man while I was waiting for help."

He nodded and smiled a smile that went all the way to his eyes. The first smile she'd seen on his otherwise, solemn face. This Gabriel was a handsome man, she decided, but he could only distract her from her pain for so long.

"How bad is it, doctor?"

CHAPTER 3

"You have a broken leg."

Slowly and delicately he ran his hand along the break and tears rolled down her face.

"But it doesn't feel like the bone is shattered. It's a clean break. No protruding bone. You should heal okay, Miss Moore."

She let out a sigh of relief and thankfulness filled her being.

"Is someone in your family meeting you in Cracker City?"

"No. I'm on my way to Haines. To be a teacher," she said through clenched teeth, wondering how she was going to move about with all this pain.

Gabriel looked back at the mules and as if deep in thought he rose slowly, grabbed her bag and headed to them.

This Gabriel Stone wore boots that went up to his knees, but loose around the ankles, not fitted. His hat had a wide brim that sloped down in the back, whether by design or from wear she didn't know. He'd rolled up the sleeves of his wool, blue shirt and a gun with a curved handle was belted low on his waist.

Gabriel brought back two boards and put one on each side of her leg, then carefully wrapped strips of sheets around her leg and boards. After testing the sprint for solidarity, he picked her up as easily as if she weighed as much as a child.

As he turned, her head took a spin and she giggled with glee. “I believe I’m a little tipsy.”

“Yes, you just might be, but a stable sprint is probably adding to your happiness, too.”

When Gabriel smiled, Isabella looked at his full lips and even white teeth, then up to the crow’s feet around brilliant blue eyes. The man was downright fine-looking. The thought made her burst out in giggles again.

“What’s so funny?”

“I think you are an angel, Gabriel. Get it? The angel, Gabriel.”

“Humph. Hardly.”

“Well, you’re my angel.”

“I want you to hold tight around my neck, because I’m going to mount this mule with you in one arm. Do you think you can do that?”

“I can definitely put my arms around your neck.”

“There, did that hurt?”

“What hurt? Oh, ha, ha, my leg? It’s not moving thanks to the sprint. Doing good, doing good.”

“You don’t have to hang on so tight now. Be careful with my hat.”

“Oh, yeah.” She’d accidentally pushed it back far enough that she could see dark hair loosely curled at the nape of his neck.

“There. I’m sorry I have to hold you so close like this, Miss Moore, but I don’t think you can manage on the other mule by yourself.”

“It’s okay; I still have my gun under my skirt.”

"Oh, that's where it went, huh?"

"Hic. Yes. You best be careful," she said, but tightened her grip around his neck again.

Gabriel supposed he could have rigged something up with thick branches to pull her back to town on, but he usually only used that kind of setup in severe cases. He knew she could stand a ride in front of him on the mule, especially since he'd sat her side saddle, braced between his body and the neck of the mule. *Yet, what would he have done if she were a he?* he asked himself. It didn't matter, women were the frailer sex.

Now, as she tightened her arms around his neck, he wondered if he'd made the right decision. His mouth went dry. Even though he rarely imbibed, he reached down to his pocket and took a sip of whiskey from the flask.

"I need another drink, too," she said. When he hesitated, she stuck out her cracked bottom lip.

He slid the bottle back into his pocket. Let's wait and see if you need more later."

She pawed at his pocket, missing the area by some inches. "Whoa, it's not there! Put your hands in your lap, not mine. Looks like I need the gun."

Isabella smiled, feeling more flirtatious than she'd ever felt before. Hadn't her friend Marie told her that a woman could make advances? Why did men get to have all the fun? "See if you can find it."

"Miss Moore, you better watch yourself. Looks like laudanum would be the better choice for you. You'd at least be easier to handle."

"Hic. You're no fun."

"A gentleman treats a woman with respect."

"You act very mature. How old are you anyway?"

"I'm twenty-seven."

"You seem older somehow," she said, eyes squinting.

He knew it was true. "Uh … the war made me old."

Gabriel watched Isabella's facial features go from giddiness to sadness instantly, no doubt due to the alcohol. Her split, bottom lip trembled.

"That is so sad Gab … angel. I'm so-o-o sorry you had to fight in the war."

"I didn't fight. I was a doctor, remember?"

She nodded in a circle. "Yes. You were practicing."

He couldn't help but smile.

"I like seeing you smile. Hey! I will make you smile, take away your sadness."

"Yeah, that'll help," he said to placate her.

Darkness had fallen, plus Isabella kept blocking his view, making it nigh impossible to see where his mule headed. Her arm tightened around his neck like a snake, making her nose to nose with him. He grabbed at his hat in time to save it.

The attention of the beautiful woman made a little balloon of happiness rise in his chest. Yes, she momentarily made him forget about everything, even the war.

He couldn't help thinking about kissing her, but she beat him to it. Her ample lips touched his softly; however, she seemed unsure of how to use them. The metallic taste of blood from her injured lip reached the tip of his tongue.

She pulled away slightly. "I've never been drunk before," she whispered as if revealing a secret.

"I figured that. Be careful with your bottom lip there."

"I've never kissed a man. Only boys. Boys," she said again, in disgust. "I want a man."

Gabriel tensed at her words, surprised at what the alcohol did to this young woman. It made her impulsive and he liked it a little too much.

"You look so serious. Oh, do I frighten you? Remember if you want protection, you'll have to find my gun."

"You know, Miss Moore, you probably aren't going to remember this in the morning."

"My name is Isabella. Say it."

"Isabella, I'll say it one more time, be good so that you won't be ashamed in the morning."

"Why does everyone tell me to be good all the time?"

Her words scared him and thrilled him all at the same time. "The problem is, I will remember what you say, Isabella."

"You can call me Bella if you'd like. Hic. Bella, Bella, Bella."

He sighed. "I will remember, Bella."

"Oh, I like how you say my name."

"Why don't you lean your head right here on my chest, uh … Bella?"

"Oh, how romantic, Gabriel. Gabriel, Gabriel, Gabriel," she said, rubbing her head against his chest.

In less than a minute she was asleep, just as he'd hoped.

He looked forward, and then turned the mule around to head for town.

CHAPTER 4

Isabella was a playful little vamp, at least when she drank whiskey. Gabriel looked down at her red hair, then touched a loose strand with a thumb and forefinger. Silky and soft, like the rest of her lying against him.

He'd become a numb man, he knew. Somehow life became easier that way; life was tolerable if you didn't have to feel anything. But this woman made him want to feel, to experience more than just seeing the color in his dreary, gray, lackluster life.

It had been awhile since he'd kissed a girl, didn't think he'd missed it that much until today. Part of him wished he'd not met her, so that he could go on with life as he'd made it.

Yet, he told himself he was ready for change. Wasn't that why he'd gone west to the wilderness, to find himself, understand himself and move on?

All he'd ever dreamed about was becoming a doctor, to help people be healthy. Sure, he'd had successes, but they didn't measure up to the piles of body parts he'd amassed outside of operating tents during the war.

He sighed and Isabella moved slightly. The problem literally at hand was what he should be thinking about. There wasn't a decent woman in town to help her, but would it be proper if he took her home to care for her? He supposed he had time to think about it as he headed home in the dark. A darkness that would hide her from the town's people until someone came calling.

Isabella awoke when Gabriel shifted her off the mule. She winced and held her breath for a moment.

"I'll give you a little more whiskey after I get you settled for the night."

"I need an outhouse," she said, looking about in the moon light.

"Certainly."

They managed to make it to the porch in the dark. Gabriel shuffled her to the steps so he could light a lantern. Isabella ended up carrying the beam of light as he carried her in bridegroom fashion.

At the outhouse door, she balanced on one leg, as if wondering how she'd get inside.

"Here, let me help you."

He lifted her around the waist with one hand, then pulled the door open with the other. The sprint kept the door ajar. Her hand met his as he tried to lift her skirt and she looked at him. Her sense of propriety had returned. "The whiskey is wearing off. You should be able to steady yourself better."

A moment before he turned, his eyes caught the gun strapped in lace to her thigh. He knew she meant for him to see it, a reminder that she wasn't defenseless.

Gabriel, holding Isabella, headed to the door of his log cabin.

"I'm impressed," she said, holding the lantern up to get a better view. "Nice cabin."

Gabriel could feel the rush of blood to his face. He was proud of the work he'd done cutting logs, peeling the bark off, and stacking them with a mixture of chink to hold them together.

"Thank you."

After balancing Isabella, Gabriel lit another lantern, helped her inside, and shut curtains made of dishcloths. The room smelled of fresh hewn wood. An old broom leaned against the corner.

"I don't think we need a fire tonight." He'd fashioned his fireplace hearth out of stone. Attached was an iron apparatus that he could swing back and forth to roast meat.

The square cabin had no separate bedroom or kitchen area, just a corner for each. A bowl and pitcher set on a table next to a bed that looked more practical than soft, like a wooden bunk with a layer of blankets and quilts on it.

Gabriel sat her down on one foot and she leaned on the rectangular, rustic wood table and put a hand on the back of one of the two chairs.

She took a seat and looked down at her leg, then at Gabriel. He poured her a shot of whiskey. His expression made her think that he was the one wounded. "This will help you get through the cast I plan to put on your leg."

She watched him gather supplies from a cupboard, taking his time, considering each item he picked up. Starting to feel comfortable, she sighed and then watched how the light caught his chestnut hair at different angles.

Finally he was in front of her, frowning, dabbing a cloth in a watery liquid and then wiping her cracked lip. Even though her lip stung, she couldn't take her eyes off his perpetual scowl.

His sullen look perplexed her. Wasn't he supposed to encourage his patients? Instead it was as if all the vivacity was sucked from the cabin. "You seem a very serious man, Gabriel."

He took a chair across from her. "I suppose I am. My

youth is gone, Isabella," he said matter-of-factly, as if this was how it was going to be.

"Not at twenty-seven."

"I believe we've gone over this before."

She believed people were never too old to change their lives. "For one, you need to smile more. You have a beautiful smile."

He gave her a half smile when she put her elbow on the table and set her chin in her hand. "There you go. Bea-u-ti-ful."

"You're forgetting you will be sorry for some of the things you've said to me."

She shook her wobbly head. "I didn't say anything I didn't mean, I'm sure."

"You need to lie down on the table," Gabriel said in his most professional tone of voice. "But first - "

Inside her bag he found a nightshirt and helped her change clothes. He covered her body as much as he could with a sheet, which at times became cumbersome as it mixed with her clothes. To slow the process even more, she stiffened when he touched a sore spot or moved her foot and leg too much.

He did his best to cocoon her in a blanket, so that her body would be still, and had her lie down on the only bed in the room.

"These are cardboard splints and bandages. I'm going to soak them in a solution of what is called dextrin and then I will apply it to your leg while it's wet. The problem with a cast is that your movements will be restricted." Gabriel looked at her then, and she suspected there was something he wasn't telling her.

"What else?"

"You have to be as still as you can for six hours while the cast dries."

"Six *hours?*"

"Well, some still use starch instead of dextrin to make a cast, which takes two to three days to dry. It should be dry by morning."

She nodded.

"Now that I'm giving you the bad news, bed rest is the best cure."

A tear slipped down her face and in vain she turned her face to the side to hide it. After a moment of silent crying, she blurted out, "My jo-o-ob."

He took an oversized pillow and placed it behind her head and neck. "You just need some time and you will be good as new. I'll help you get situated so that you can get a good night's sleep. Lord knows you need it."

"Hotel? Are you taking me to a hotel?"

"No, you need to stay here tonight. I'll keep an eye on you. I don't want you moving while the cast dries. Tomorrow we can talk about what you should do."

She nodded and reached out to him, like a trusting little girl to her father, and it struck something in him. It was a pang, a quickening of some hardened emotion.

"I'll give you one more swig of whiskey to help get you to sleep. Here, raise your head as much as you can."

Her eyes followed him as he moved about the room, and then felt the cool, wet strips of material that he applied over and over her leg. After a while, his movements became comforting. That's the last thing she remembered.

When Gabriel returned from tending the mules, Isabella lay sleeping. The gashed, swollen lip looked so foreign on her peaches and cream complexion. As he watched her breathe, he felt like a child bringing home a lost puppy, hoping he could keep it.

"Don't get too attached," he said in a whisper, before finding a place on the floor to sleep.

CHAPTER 5

"Feel like you've been in a stagecoach accident?"

Isabella opened her eyes to see Gabriel hovering over her. Not surprising, he wore his wrinkled brow like the weight of the world was on his shoulders.

She figured she didn't look much better. "Is that all that happened? I feel like I was cast off a mountain side and rolled to the bottom. Why does my head hurt so much?" she asked, hands to her face.

"Whiskey, plus a few bumps."

"Oh, yeah," she said and rubbed her forehead.

"Do you remember much about last night?" He waited on bated breath, so she made every effort to think back.

"I remember you bringing me here, uh … instead of a hotel, so you could keep an eye on me."

"So I could help you."

She nodded. "Thanks by the way, Gabriel. Angel Gabriel."

If possible, his frown deepened. He was such a serious, proper man who could surely benefit from a little teasing. So she searched even harder through her memories.

"Oh, and you kissed me."

"Correction, you kissed me," he said, a finger pointed at her.

"Don't be so serious, we both lived through it."

His lips went to a straight line and he moved toward the door. "Here's a crutch made out of the stoutest limb I could find. See if you can stand, so I can cut the limb to the right height."

She winced making an effort to stand. Now, with a clear mind, she wondered what she'd do to take care of herself on a daily basis, let alone get back on the stage to Haines.

Gabriel took her measure and marked the crutch with a knife.

"I'll be right back. I'm going outside to saw it to fit. I'll give you some time to get dressed. Can you manage?"

She nodded and moved herself to a sitting position. Before she worried too much, she decided to see how well she could get along with the crutch.

The cocoon of blankets and her pillow fell to the floor. With great effort, she moved her body and her new cast to her bag and pulled out her gray dress. She scanned it for damage and found the rip at the hem was repairable, but it'd have to wait for another day. Her other everyday dress would have to suffice for awhile, she decided and pulled it over her head.

"You can come in now!"

"Here you go," he said, tapping the crunch on the floor. Let's see how you can maneuver to the outhouse."

"I'll try my best," she said to Gabriel as well as to herself.

"Don't put any weight on it."

"I don't think I can anyway. No, I can't," she said, then took in a breath and grimaced.

After only a few steps, Gabriel had to help her, to steady her as she walked.

A tear slipped down her face and dropped on her cast.

She'd told herself for some time that she could handle whatever the Wild West could hand her, but didn't foresee this type of thing at all. Suddenly, she wasn't an independent woman, but nearly as helpless as a baby.

She tried to hide her tears, ashamed to let Gabriel know the extent of her distress, but it didn't work.

"Sorry about the pain," he said. "Remember I have some laudanum if it's too bad."

She sniffed. "It's not only that. I'm upset because I have plans and - "

He stood behind her and stopped any movement by taking the tops of her arms in his hands. "I can tell you that you will heal. At your young age you should be as good as new in five to six weeks, but be mobile far before that."

She turned her head as far as she could toward him. "And until then? I may not be able to keep my job nor am I physically able to go home." After a moment she said, "I have some money, is there someone in town that could take care of me?"

He sighed, and she pressed her lips together, waiting for bad news.

"As of this morning, there isn't anyone suitable to help you, but new people are coming through all the time."

Perhaps some of Gabriel's unhappiness had to do with being saddled with her. Would he cast her to the wolves? Her stomach clenched in fear, drying her tears. What would happen to her? She waited in silence for more hard news.

Yet he didn't say anything, just let go of her arms and they continued on to the outhouse. Perhaps it was a good thing, because she couldn't find the words to ask for charity.

"Once you turn around, move the crutch to the good side and lean on it as you lift your … your skirt to sit down."

What usually took only a few minutes, took triple the time today due to the pain and the cumbersome cast. When the door opened, she literally fell into Gabriel's arms. With ease he brought her to standing and going with the crutch on her right side. Traveling the short journey back, she sweat like she was hiking uphill at a brisk pace.

"Do you want the laudanum?" he asked inside.

"What about the whiskey?" she asked.

His eyes widened. "Uh … the whiskey makes you move around too much."

Momentarily, she wondered at his startled expression, but then thought he was probably only afraid she'd kiss him again.

"Even though I'd like to forget about my predicament, and laudanum could help me with that, I'll not go that route. Thanks anyway."

He nodded. "Do you have any family that can come help you?"

"I have lots of family," she said, her voice rising of it's own accord. "I don't want them to say I told you so and haul me back home. I'm down but not out."

Gabriel successfully withstood a great many things in his time, but still had trouble watching a lady cry and she was about to turn on the tears again. He decided to give her some space and left the cabin for a walk.

A new resident of Cracker City, he came to the wilderness to find gold, but more importantly to come to grips with his past and future. The war had wounded him, not physically but mentally. He grew weary of wounded flesh and blood, destruction, and sickness. Even the word "doctor" conjured horrid images to mind. He didn't know if he wanted to continue being a physician, the word he used to think of himself now.

Physician, heal thyself. Recognizing the irony, his mirthless laugh rang out in the forest.

Once in Cracker City, he decided he'd practice medicine to a minimum. Not a heartless man, he'd help the injured men of the area, and then it was up to the men of the town to decide how the injured would recover. Women of consequence were another matter, but would be few and far between, and certainly wouldn't be traveling alone. Not once did he think he would be using his cabin for a sick bed for more than a day or two. He shook his head at his foolishness, for not thinking things through.

Yes, up to now he'd had a professional relationship with every patient he'd ever treated. Yet, finding a beautiful, colorful wildflower where none stood before, like an omen from above, was hard not to seize and nourish oneself with.

Isabella kissed him. He knew she was under the influence of alcohol and he let her. Now, it was neigh impossible to get that professional relationship back, making it imperative that she be cared for by someone else. Perhaps a handful of miners would agree to tend to her, but not with the right motives. Yet, if he couldn't get her to receive help from her family, he had no choice but to help her until she could help herself.

Gabriel turned back to the cabin. Being a healthy male, his heart lifted at the thought of having Isabella around even though she posed a threat to logical thinking, but what else could he do?

ISABELLA'S HAND rubbed the cast over her shin bone as Gabriel walked in the door.

"How are you doing?"

"Oh, I've had better days."

"I imagine you have. We need to talk."

Before answering, Isabella looked at Gabriel's face. His lips kept from falling into a frown by freezing into a straight line. She turned her head away in embarrassment as it became clear that her kisses last night were not appreciated and wasted on someone without a sense of humor.

She nodded, and then gave him eye contact.

"It seems to me you have but two choices," he said and stopped as if to let the words sink in.

Isabella only knew of one choice and that was to write or telegraph for her family to rescue her. She didn't want to return home with her tail between her legs. From thereafter she'd probably be shackled to a bedpost so she wouldn't run off again. A dash of hope sprung from within at this second choice.

"I'm not sure I understand. Can you tell me what my choices are?"

"You could get someone from home to come and get you, which I'm sure would be the best solution."

She shook her head vigorously.

"Then you have no choice but to stay here with me," he said grimly, as if he'd told her the end of the world would be tomorrow.

She wasn't stupid, she knew he didn't really want to help her but felt obliged. But it suited her for the moment.

Good. She'd think about how all this would work later. Keeping her face down so Gabriel wouldn't detect the joy in her countenance, Isabella said as meekly as she could, "Thank you very much, Gabriel. I'd like to stay here."

"Okay."

Isabella couldn't look at him, didn't want to see any disappointment in his eyes. Instead, she looked inward, feeling her fears subside like a popped balloon. Perhaps now she could still follow her dreams after a minimal time of healing.

Looking around the room, she wondered what to do with her time. She couldn't help but notice the makeshift divider that Gabriel spread across the center of the room and wondered if she could make it more uniform. Her eyes scanned the antiques, for a lack of a better word, situated about the cabin. Some of the items not only looked old but, appeared to be hand-hewn as well. Her eyes stopped on a stack of books. From her advantage they looked more like manuals than novels.

Gabriel apparently caught her looking at the bookshelf and held up a newspaper. "There are two newspapers in this town. One tells the truth, while the other is full of lies to sell mines around here. Which would you prefer to read?"

"Really? Someone would do that?"

He nodded. "A man named Brown."

"And nobody is stopping him?"

"Not yet."

"I'll take the honest one."

She was thankful to have anything to read or do. Soon bored, she found herself staring at Gabriel's gloomy profile, as he busied himself about the cabin, or looked outside the window. She longed to make him smile again, to make the sadness go away, but didn't know how.

He turned toward her. "Here is paper, pen and ink, so that you can write to your family."

"Maybe I should read Brown's newspaper, too, so I'll have something interesting to tell them," she said, hoping to make him smile.

He gave her a half smile in return, but it was something, enough to challenge her into getting more.

She looked down at the blank sheet. Her plan was to notify her parents after she made it to her teaching job and situated in the home of her employer. Gabriel was right, she needed to tell them something, but instead decided to write her prospective employer to tell them of her setback, with a plan to come later.

~

OLINA MOORE STOOD on the top step of the porch, eyes straining, hoping to catch sight of her only daughter in the distance.

"Isabella can be so impulsive. She acted without really thinking this out," she said with a shake of her head.

Her husband stepped closer, put a hand on the porch rail, and looked out as well. "Yes, I suppose she's had to be to survive a house full of brothers. You know, she can grab a drumstick faster than any of them and move to the front of a line full of muscle to not miss anything going on."

She bit her lip. "John, are we to blame for her leaving home like she did?"

He sighed. "I've wondered that too, but I think she is reckless because of her environment. She's watched and listened to her brothers coming of age and choosing what they want to do with their lives. It's another thing she wants to take part in, even though she knows that women have fewer opportunities."

"Perhaps she wouldn't have thought about opportunity if it weren't for her friend, Marie," said Olina, bitterly. "Marie has to think about equality, because she has no other choice but to be an old maid. She's totally behind that new American Equal Rights Association and now she's put foolish notions into our daughter's head. I believe she already has choices; there's not a young man around who hasn't tried to woo Bella. To be a wife of a successful man in this town is reward in itself."

John nodded and then rubbed his forehead. "Looking back now, I see how she prepared to leave by taking long walks to get us used to her not being around. And never has a horse been so cared for than hers."

Olina scanned the vastness in front of her again. "And spending time remaking older dresses to fit current trends, just to fold them and stack them in the closet. I thought to ask her about that but didn't."

After a quiet moment, she added, "She'd talked of leaving Prairie City to teach school, but I thought she'd get over it when we had nothing good to say about her leaving town. I didn't realize the extent of her desire and stubbornness, John, and I never thought she'd go off on her own."

John nodded.

"And just who is chosen to bring us her good-bye note? Marie!" Olina turned to her husband and cried on his shoulder. At length she asked, "What if something happens to her?"

He put his hands on her shoulders. "Well, we know she won't go down without a fight. You can ask her brothers about that," he added with a forced smile.

After giving him an absent look, she asked, "What are we going to do to get our only daughter back?

"Now, don't you worry. The note said she needs a little time, and as soon as she lets us know where she's at, we'll go get her."

CHAPTER 6

After a nap, Gabriel helped Isabella to the outhouse and back.

"You did a nice job building this cabin," she said for the second time upon entering.

Gabriel smiled. He simply smiled; she didn't expect it.

"Is this the first cabin you've built?"

"No, it's the second. The first was trial and error and a good learning experience. I like how this one turned out. Thanks."

Gabriel stoked the fire, which felt good on a cold mountain morning. He told her the final embers would last until the sun shone overhead and heated the day to eighty degrees or above. When the sun went down, the cold rushed in once more.

He stared into the flames seemingly miles away in thought. She so wanted to know his thoughts and wondered if it was because of boredom or her attraction to a handsome man.

"Do you have any family left?"

As if shocked she was still in the same room with him, he

moved quickly nearly hitting his head on the hearth. "I have a mother, father, and sister in Illinois."

"Are they well?"

"Yes. Yes."

"Illinois? The birthplace of Abraham Lincoln."

"It's one claim to fame."

After a moment, she asked, "Do you think you'll ever go back to Illinois?"

He looked truly puzzled when he said, "I don't know."

"You're not wanted by the law are you? In Illinois," she asked with a lilt in her voice.

He looked her square in the eye and gave her a slow half smile, as if it was an effort to make his frown turn upside down. "No."

An almost smile was better than nothing, she decided. Still, she gave him a full smile and he returned it. Her heart fluttered, which surprised her. She didn't know a smile could go to her head like that.

"One of the reasons I came out west was to decide what I want to do with my life, where to go."

"Perhaps you need a woman to tell you where to go, where to live," she said tongue-in-cheek.

Gabriel not only smiled but laughed. "Well, I didn't know it could be as simple as that."

"That's what my brother says anyway."

After a quiet moment, Gabriel said, "You must be involved with women's suffrage, huh?"

"Where did you get that idea?" she asked, dumbfounded.

"You're a woman traveling alone and are fine with it."

"Well, let's just say this trip is what I would call my declaration of independence."

"Oh?" Gabriel looked a little concerned and she couldn't blame him.

"Independence from doting parents and six brothers who don't think I can do one thing without their help."

"You sound a little bitter."

"I'm not. Well ... maybe. It's just that I'm twenty-one years old and it's high time I do what I want."

"Most women I know are married by the time they're twenty-one. Maybe that's why you came to a land infested with men."

Since she couldn't very well stand up to make her point, she put a hand on a hip. "How absurd! I am not feeling a need to get married. I really do want to accomplish a few things in my life. Is that so bad?"

"It depends if it's dangerous or not, I suppose."

"Please, you're sounding like a brother." She shook her head. "I want to be a teacher and was in the process of doing just that."

Gabriel stood up. "Aren't there any teaching jobs closer to where you live?"

"There could be, yes, but I happen to want to try my hand at finding gold, too." When his eyebrows furrowed, she added, "Why not?"

"It's too hard of a job for a woman."

"Panning. I can pan for gold, without too much muscle, Gabriel. I just have to learn, is all."

He pointed a finger at her, then squinted one eye. "But out here you're in the midst of some of the rowdiest bunch of characters in the states."

"I can shoot. I've had hours of practice shooting a gun."

Gabriel crossed his arms. "Tell me this, then. Do you plan to just wave your gun around to scare them, which I doubt will work? Or maim, paralyze or shoot to kill?"

She frowned. "Why should you care?"

"Because I will most likely have to treat some of these fellows," he said, palms up.

Isabella looked down at her feet, deep in thought. When she learned to shoot, her goal was to focus on accuracy, not whether she had to kill somebody. She supposed she was naïve enough at the time to think a waving gun would stop trouble. After she fell from the stage, she only thought about killing a wild animal if it tried to eat her. Could she kill someone if she had to? Gabriel was right; she needed to think this through.

Isabella looked up. "What did you say?"

"I said, do you think you can actually kill somebody? Live with yourself after cutting someone's number of days?"

"I suppose I can to protect someone I love. I don't know," she answered, looking down, shaking her head.

"Perhaps you need to spend some of your down time thinking about this," he suggested with a firm, no nonsense voice.

Gabriel left the cabin, seemingly frustrated. Now she added something else to his unhappiness. She didn't want that.

She supposed it was simple really. If she intended to stay in the Wild West then she'd have to be prepared to deal with the cost of protecting herself, no matter the outcome.

Isabella's naiveté concerned him. She was not the independent woman she wanted to portray herself to be. She wanted to pan for gold, for goodness sake. Sure, she'd have a host of admirers waiting in line to help her in any way, and then there'd be brawls over her. Isabella couldn't stay in Cracker City for more reasons than one, not to mention that he enjoyed her company too much. Yet, how could he convince her to go back home when she could travel?

Gabriel came back in after hunting. "I shot supper.

Turkeys are in the area right now. They're kind of tough, but they're food."

"Wish I could be more helpful and I'm dying to go outside. Maybe, I can help pluck it, if you set me up so my leg won't move."

He nodded. "I'll let you help a little bit."

After he moved two chairs outdoors, he came to get her. He pulled her to standing, and then carried her outside. When they were face to face, she said, "I wish you would smile more, Gabriel."

"I am smiling." He wasn't.

His comment made her smile so big it exposed both layers of her white teeth. Her green eyes danced, and he wanted to put a hand in her hair. It was impossible not to grin back like some sort of fool.

"You are such a handsome man when you smile, Gabriel. You nearly take my breath away."

He shook his head. "You shouldn't say that, Bella."

"I like the sound of my name when you say it."

He frowned, as he sat her on one chair and propped her leg on the other. "I'm your doctor."

"So you are," she said lightheartedly. "Let's get to work on that turkey."

Her mother told her she spoke before thinking many times. She'd done that just now, but she didn't really care because she made Gabriel smile again. To put a smile back on his face was what she wanted, she told herself, but she knew it was more than that. Yes, she wanted to kiss him again, too, and this time not under the influence of whiskey. Quite frankly, she had a crush on him.

He'd stripped off both shirts and let the sun beat on his back as he plucked the turkey with experienced hands. Mesmerized, she watched the ripple of the muscles in his arms and shoulders while he worked. A sprinkling of chest hair formed an upside-down triangle. Even though she'd grown up with a lot of brothers, it was the first occasion she'd really took the time to notice a man before.

She didn't do much to pluck this bird, but she felt good about giving a little something back to Gabriel. She didn't like being a burden on anyone, but knew she had no choice.

Each day, Gabriel left the house. Today, he prepared to leave again. He put his feet into heavy boots and buttoned his blue wool shirt over an undershirt.

She couldn't stand the thought that maybe she was responsible for his absence. He was a man of few words, so he didn't really offer any information, just that he'd be back by such and such time. Worried that he left on her account, she finally dared to ask him.

"Gabriel, where are you going?"

He looked at her in surprise. "I have to make a living, you know."

Oh, it all made sense now. He did come home dirty. "Are you mining for gold?" she asked, with probably too much excitement, because his lips drew a thin line.

He shook his head. "I've tried mining and it's hard and dangerous work, too much so for me. Still, I've been able to get a nugget or two from miners who've been patients. I'm trying to find a job I'm happy with."

Finding a new job didn't surprise her; she knew he thought seriously about leaving the medical field. "What are you doing then?"

"I'm a blacksmith. The owner of the shop wants some time to find gold himself, so I asked if I could fill in for him."

"Humph." He didn't seem any happier when he came home from this job. "My father said that the job of blacksmith may die out soon."

"For now they are needed here in the West, especially in mining communities. Wages are good here."

He grabbed his hat and left with a nod of his head.

Isabella couldn't be any more bored, so she searched through Gabriel's bookcase for something to read, through his books, volumes of notes and medical periodicals. She grabbed two periodicals and hopped back to a chair.

She looked up and frowned. Something moved outside but didn't sound as heavy-footed as a man. She cringed remembering a rat that had stowed itself under her family home. When the lights went out at night, she could hear them moving under the floor. The memory made her focus on her reading, pushing down any interest in seeing what the creature could be.

"Have you seen any rats around here?" she asked as soon as Gabriel returned home. He sat down a bucket of water before turning to look at her.

"Yes, there are rats around here. I've not seen any, only mice, snakes, spiders."

"Thanks, that was comforting."

He almost smiled. "Why do you ask?"

"Oh, I heard something outside, thought maybe it was a pack rat."

"It could be a pack rat. I've heard they're actually very cute. Gray with white boots and a furry tail."

She frowned in reply. "I still don't want to see it."

CHAPTER 7

Each night, Isabella listened for Gabriel to fall asleep. Even though he'd put up a room divider, she could hear a pin drop on the other side. Hardly a night passed that he didn't toss and turn, first. Tonight, he was especially restless.

"I've been reading through your bookcase. I hope that's okay," she said to the ceiling.

"Sorry, I don't have anything more enjoyable for you to read."

"Actually, I'm finding it more interesting than I thought I would. I can't believe how many bones are in our bodies."

"I've memorized most of them."

"Okay then. What is the smallest bone in the human body and where is it?" she asked.

"Stapes. It's in the ear."

"I'm impressed.

"Aren't you going to ask me what it does? Okay, I'll tell you - "

"No. No. Me! Me!" She raised her hand even though he couldn't see it.

"Okay. Go ahead."

"The belief is that it transmits sound vibrations," she said quickly and laughed with glee. "Okay, okay. I have a question for you."

He chuckled and she took it to heart. "I'd like to kick you in the coccyx. Now I might be saying it wrong, but what is a coccyx?"

"Well, my bottom is not bone, so, I'll have to say the tail bone."

She giggled again. Her hands folded on her chest, eyes toward the ceiling. "I don't really want to kick your tail bone."

"Well, that's a relief."

She smiled in the darkness, waiting for him to say something else. When he didn't, she let out a breath and tried to make herself comfortable for the night.

"Bella?"

"Hmm?"

"You really don't find the books boring?" he finally asked.

"They're interesting. I think I can understand your interest in medicine now."

Gabriel sighed and it sounded almost contented. A sound she'd not heard from him before. She believed it meant he still had an interest in medicine. Her last thought of the night was a prayer to God that Gabriel could find this something more he was set on looking for.

GABRIEL TURNED to look at Isabella. "Next week will be two weeks since your accident and you're gaining strength. I think I'll take you to Main Street, let you look around Cracker City."

"Oh, will you? I'm stir crazy, in case you haven't noticed."

He nodded. "Yes, I've noticed."

"If my leg can handle this, will you take me gold panning? I can at least watch you if I can't do anything else."

He frowned. "We'll see."

She didn't want to have to beg, but she was in a mining district and so wanted to try her hand at it.

GABRIEL DIDN'T THINK he'd ever seen such a beautiful sight. Isabella was a vision in green. She'd twisted her red hair up on her head, but a few curls dropped onto the ivory skin of her neck and shoulders. A small green hat nestled on top of her head and came to a V at her forehead. Due to the cast, she had one shoe on and one shoe off.

After taking a moment to appreciate her beauty, he said, "Why are you dressed like that? We're just going down Main Street."

She frowned. "This is the type of dress I would wear into town. What's wrong with it?"

"Nothing, it's just that you'll get a lot of attention. Is that what you want?" The serious look in his eye disturbed her.

With a hand on her waist, and the other on her crutch, she answered, "Are you thinking I'm out to get attention on purpose? Is that it?"

"You won't even have to try. Are you ready for that?"

Her furrowed brow told him no, but she said, "Yes, of course. I'd like to see what a mining town is all about. Don't worry about me. I have a gun under my skirt."

He forced himself not to conjure up the image for a second time. After a shake of his head, he said, "A gun can get you killed."

When she didn't reply, only shook her head, he said, "Okay, then, I'll get a mule." And *my* gun, he thought grimly.

Yet, despite the danger, he wanted her to see what being one of the only decent women in town felt like. He hoped that the experience would send her packing for home where she belonged.

ISABELLA LOOKED down at her dress. Who was she kidding? She'd dressed for Gabriel and no one else.

By now, she could move more freely on her crutch. Gabriel allowed independence as much as he could but was within reach in case the uneven ground became too difficult to maneuver.

Because of her feelings for Gabriel, she clung tighter than she needed to when he picked her up and set her on top of the mule. She sat sidesaddle and firmly hung onto the saddle on both sides. When Gabriel was satisfied, he led the mule down the terraces the town was built on.

The cool of the morning had dissipated and now the sun above felt good on her shoulders. Pine and fir trees, rocky knolls and high peaks surrounded her.

She so looked forward to seeing Cracker City. Due to her unfortunate state on the day she arrived, she didn't really see the town.

"This is Little Cracker Creek which runs into Cracker Creek over there," said Gabriel, pointing. It was hard to hear because of the water rushing over the rocks. "The mansion beyond Little Cracker Creek there belongs to Brown."

Brown was the carpetbagger he'd told her about, she remembered. "Looks like he's very successful."

Between the pines, firs, and cottonwoods, Isabella spotted men panning for gold along the bank and boulders of Cracker Creek. She watched them as they passed by, until her neck couldn't turn anymore.

Isabella decided right then, that as soon as she was able to foot it down to the creek, she'd come to watch and then learn to pan herself. A little bubble of happiness filled her, as she'd soon be able to try something she'd only dreamed of.

The town consisted of a main street crowded with buildings. Isabella noted the newspaper offices, saloons, general store and a hotel. Tents and cabins filled the terraces above the main street.

A boardwalk was along one side of Main, and stumps were still standing here and there along the edges giving her a personal account of what a "stump town" looked like.

From a distance, Isabella could see people lining up, waiting for something. The closer they came she saw so many men that she wondered if any were left in the mines.

"Gabriel?"

His eyes followed hers. "The men are waiting in line for the stage to arrive. Remember the mail comes on the stage."

She nodded.

"Mail from home is more important than anything in Cracker City. That's why the long line. To get a place in the front of the line, you have to wait for some time."

"I hope their wait isn't wasted."

"Well, that's the thing. Around here, if you don't hear from someone in a timely manner, the more likely you are to get into trouble."

As they passed by the men, all manner of conversation stopped and their eyes were on her, staring with critical interest, like she was a creature from outer space.

Now, besides the noise of the creek in the background, all she heard was the sound of the mule's footsteps as they slowly moved on. A shiver went up her spine.

"Why are they staring so? I know they've seen a woman before," she leaned toward Gabriel and asked.

He stopped the mule and stepped to her. With a quiet

voice, he said, "Their eyes are hungry. To some you are a reminder of a sister, or friend, or mother. To others you are a woman of class, they'd like to get to know better. To others you are a sexual object that they need. I don't advise encouraging them with a smile. Look ahead."

She felt her face redden in embarrassment. He offered no apologies for the coarse words, only started walking again. Sharp whistles and low discussions followed them.

"Where are we going first?" she said loud enough for Gabriel to hear her.

"Blacksmith's shop. I want to get a new shoe for the mule and pick up my wage. Then we'll stop by the general store and buy a few things."

CHAPTER 8

"This is my boss, Benjamin Ott," introduced Gabriel.

"How do you do?" Isabella stretched out a gloved hand and then moved it back slowly as she noticed the dirty work gloves shrouding Benjamin's hands.

"Sorry, about the dirt. How do you do?" he asked with a nod instead.

"Fine, thank you."

In the middle of the blacksmith shop rested an anvil on a thick tree stump. The hearth, with rocks in wooden cribbing, was the farthest from the door. Between the two a barrel of water was placed, plus a bucket for brine and oil. Benches and worktables, scattered with tools, filled the perimeter of the room.

"Did you see the drill steels I made over there, Ben?"

"Yes. Good job."

Gabriel pointed to a chair by the door and Benjamin swiped it with a broom before she sat down.

"You planning to work, are you?" asked Benjamin.

"I need a shoe for my mule."

"Use what's over there," Ben said, pointing with a

hammer, nodded at Isabella, and then walked back to his own work of constructing a chain.

Gabriel prepared to work on the shoe by pulling his shirt off, and then picked another shirt and an apron to work in.

Isabella hoped her staring could be interpreted as interest in Gabriel's work rather than in his muscled shoulders and arms gained from his work as a blacksmith. Her eyes trailed down to the muscled ribs above his belt.

He didn't look at her, but she noticed Ben did and she lowered her eyes in embarrassment. Suddenly the room was very hot, not only because of her flushed face, but due to the temperature in the room. She wondered how Gabriel could withstand the heat.

She watched Gabriel rhythmically progress until the shoe was finished. He looked at her and she smiled. His eyebrows shot up in question and she wondered why he didn't instantly understand that she smiled because she'd seen him accomplish something. She shook her head, meaning never mind.

When the noise died down, Gabriel said, "Like your father mentioned, the life of a blacksmith is shortened due to factories, but a constant supply of iron is needed for a mining town. We can make iron here from scrap piles in the area, where it would be costly and take weeks to be transported from somewhere else."

"And, we get a dollar more a day than the men working in the mines," added Ben.

"I NEED to start pulling my weight," Isabella said, watching Gabriel put cans of food on the counter of the general store."

"Oh? Besides being a teacher what can you do?" There was no malice in his words, only curiosity.

"I'm thinking belated spring cleaning. Your walls have black grime on them from all the winter months of burning wood. I can wash the walls down." She stood taller. "I can clean every nook and drawer and air out your mattress. Beat rugs or clean them if I can."

He gave her a half smile. "I'm impressed, but when you are well enough to do all that, then you are well enough to board the stage."

Somehow, she didn't want to hear about her leaving. Not yet. "But you have a need; your house needs cleaning."

"I can live with grimy walls, I have thus far."

"What I mean to say is that I feel like it's my responsibility to pay you back for your work and I can't really spare any of the money I have right now."

Isabella wasn't aware of the store owner's eyes and ears on them until the moment he set an extra can on the counter. A nametag with the name Earl had been pinned to his breast pocket. With a smile, Earl said, "This is good for cleaning the grime off the walls."

Isabella beamed and Gabriel sighed, but he did buy it.

As they made it out the door of the store, they were met by a good portion of Cracker City's occupants. Gabriel pulled Isabella closer to him and moved her toward the mule by way of the all-male crowd. "Excuse me. Excuse me!"

After clearing the boardwalk, she stopped to reposition her crutch, and then they moved toward the mule.

"Hey Doc?" said one man. "This ain't the same gal that was hurt on the stage is it?"

"Yes." Gabriel lifted her onto the mule with one arm and kept a hand on the handle of his gun.

"Why, no one said she was such a beauty."

"She is healing nicely," Gabriel said curtly.

The men circled the mule, giving her an eerie feeling. She felt hands on both ankles, and while thankful they didn't go farther up her leg, the touching bothered her sore leg. "Ouch!"

"Oh, sorry Miss."

"Welcome to Cracker City!" a voice sounded and then others chimed in.

"Thank you," she answered hesitantly.

Two pushed business cards in her palm, and one lifted a hat to her. Most of the others stared at her with a slack jaw.

"She's not ready to have callers, yet," Gabriel added in a loud voice. "This is her first trip out of the house."

Overwhelmed by the crowd inching toward her with hands outstretched, she didn't know what to say or do and her breath came in fast gasps. She feared someone would pull her off the mule and she'd be mauled by them all. She put her hands to her face and closed her eyes. The face of an especially trying sibling came to mind as if to remind her to get her inner courage back.

"Get back!" she yelled and kicked at those nearest her good leg. "Get … back!"

A man to the rear of her was out of reach of her kicking foot and the mule's leg. His hand moved and lingered on her bottom, even after she'd asked him to stop.

From her purse she pulled a rock that fit in her palm and swung back at the offensive man. She smiled when she heard him fall like a tree in a windstorm. Men moved toward the fallen man.

"Isabella? What did you do?" asked Gabriel leaning toward her. "I was going to pull us out of here."

"He was making improper advances."

Gabriel sighed, and then moved them away from the crowd.

Once the men figured out what happened, laughter filled the air.

"I think I'll be a doctor," said one and the group laughed again.

She was sorry about the teasing; she meant no harm to Gabriel.

"You hit him pretty hard," Gabriel said in a chastising voice.

"He'll get up in a minute."

"Oh? How do you know this? I'm the physician here."

"Because I have brothers."

Gabriel moved faster along the street. "Hitting the forehead is not good. The frontal lobe is supposed to be the center of reasoning. That's the last thing a character like that needs."

"Sorry, but I was aiming for his nose. More blood that way."

"Humph."

She tried to focus on the miners along the creek, wondering if she'd join them soon. Surely since the mail came there would be fewer men near the creek during this hour. She wondered if she could pan for gold next week.

Isabella felt good, not only because she had a day out of the house, but she now had a plan to pay Gabriel back. When he started to bring her down from the mule, she put her arms around his neck, pulled her feet together, and then slid down his body. She returned his startled look with a huge smile.

"You shouldn't do this, Isabella."

"Why not?"

"Because you're my patient."

"It doesn't matter to me what your vocation is. I like you, the man."

CHAPTER 9

How simple it was for Isabella to define him, and not even by vocation. He didn't even know himself, so how could she who had just met him but a short time ago?

"You don't really know me," he answered and took her arms from around his neck.

She jutted her lower lip in a pout, and he forced himself to think as a doctor. Okay, the lip had healed nicely.

"What's not to know?"

Gabriel didn't answer, only stuck her crutch under her arm. He helped her back toward the house.

She stopped the process, turning toward him. "I know that you are a kind person, who tries to do the right thing. Why look, you're taking care of me."

He didn't want to continue this line of thinking, this angel Gabriel thing. "Maybe it's because you are a beautiful woman. Maybe I had an ulterior motive, hm? Not that many women around here, you know."

"Sorry, can't go for that. If anything, I've been forcing myself on you."

"Well, that is not entirely, true."

She scowled at him. "What?"

He shook his head as if to clear it. "Listen, this kind of thing happens with doctors and their patients. The doctor helps the patient and then the patient thinks she's in love with him."

"Humph," she said, with chin up and tried to move toward the cabin without his help. He grabbed at her. "Let go of me!"

He did and gritted his teeth as she proceeded to limp to the cabin. She stood there and then pressed her forehead against the door.

Gabriel turned to grab the bag of groceries. Putting away the groceries would help him focus on something else, not Isabella's smile and the way her body felt pressed against his. He shook his head. If anything, it was the other way around; the doctor falling for the patient.

Isabella had beauty and brains and could have any man she wanted. Why she was still single at twenty-one was a mystery to him.

Nevertheless, she needed someone who wasn't damaged by the war, not still obsessed with it. He so wanted to move on with his life, but he kept going back and couldn't let it go. Being intimate with Isabella was not going to fix his problems, just add to them.

They hardly spoke that evening, nor made eye contact, and both turned in for bed earlier than usual.

The cabin, now divided only by the blanket, allowed him to hear her breathe before he went to sleep. Yet, tonight he couldn't focus on her breathing without feeling pain in his groin. If possible, each day he wanted her more.

"Officer, it's okay. You'll be o-kay."

"Don't take my leg. Whatever you do, don't take my leg!"

The sound of sawing in the background didn't help the situation. "We've ran out of options. If I don't amputate part of your leg, you won't be okay, you'll die from gangrene."

Tears formed in the young soldier's eyes, and he turned his head from side to side in denial. "How will I make a living without my leg? I can't imagine my wife ever wanting to touch me again."

"She'll want you alive, is what she'll want. You will be able to learn to get around again and do many of the things you used to do."

"Nooooo," he said and cried aloud, then started swinging at Gabriel.

"Gabriel! Wake up!"

HE'D BEEN TOSSING from side to side and mumbling in deep anguish. Deeply concerned, Isabella had hopped on one foot to get to his side.

"Wake up," she whispered as she put a hand on his shoulder.

He jerked awake, then grabbed her hand and took in gulps of air.

"It's just a dream," she said firmly.

"Oh," he said, recognizing her voice.

Isabella supposed she should try to move his thoughts away from the dream, but she wanted to know what bothered him so.

"Tell me, Gabriel."

"What?" he answered, still a little dazed.

"What were you dreaming about?"

He started to sit up, but her arm on his shoulder kept him down.

"You don't want to know." He rubbed his face, then added, "You should go to bed."

"I will, just as soon as you tell me what disturbed your sleep."

He chuckled, mirthlessly. "That's a nice way of saying it. What if you can't go to sleep after I tell you?"

"I never have trouble going to sleep. Even with a broken leg, remember?"

"Like I said, I was a doctor during the Civil War. I was young and idealistic and planned to save the world, plus make marvelous gains in the medical world.

"I wasn't prepared for the war. I guess I stupidly thought that I would simply patch the men up, get them healed, and then send them back in. Of course, that was true with some. For others, I had to amputate legs and watch people die from the plague.

"Many hoped this would be a 'brotherly' war, so we weren't prepared to handle supply and health needs of large armies. Disease took twice as many as battle did. Many died due to infected minor wounds.

"There was nothing I could do to make them good as new, to keep people from dying. Many were cut down far too young, never getting a chance to enjoy a long life with a wife and children or to enjoy the work of their hands. Oh, and people turned evil amongst the ravages of war, while others could blindly fight for their country no matter what."

Isabella nodded as if she understood but listened carefully trying to assimilate what was said and unsaid.

"To this day, I don't know if it was worse being a soldier or a doctor in the war." After a moment, he said so very quietly that she could barely make out the words, "The work of my hands."

He'd been facing the ceiling and now he looked at her in the dim light and tightened his hold on her hand.

He didn't tell her what he dreamed exactly, but he did feel calmer by talking about the war. He could sense that she didn't want to upset him again and didn't ask for more.

"Okay, you're right, there is a lot more to learn about you." She let go of his hand. "You're a nice man. I'm glad you didn't get the plague and die, Gabriel."

He smiled. "Thank you."

"Did you ever wonder why God let you live, when so many others died?" she added.

"Huh," was all he said.

He watched her turn, steady herself on the table, and then hop back to bed.

Gabriel thought about what Isabella said. Why had God kept him alive? He had every opportunity to get sick with smallpox or typhoid, more so than others. Other people had asked him the same thing, but he'd always told them he was too busy to get sick. Surprisingly, he'd never considered any other option until now. Maybe because it was hard to see God in a war zone, a place where it didn't seem that He heard the cries of pain and helplessness. Gabriel wondered just when he stopped believing in a caring God.

Before he went to sleep, he thought about the God of his youth. In earnest he summoned the young man that heartily believed in the words of the Bible. Suddenly, like it was yesterday, he remembered his baptism. He also recalled talking to his parents about going into medicine. His mother had declared that his job in medicine could very well be a God-given gift. He believed it then, but the question remained, did he believe it now?

CHAPTER 10

A flash of lightening lit the sky, followed by a boom of thunder that sounded so loud that Isabella jumped. "Oh, my."

"Yes, we have some amazing storms around here," Gabriel said with a nod towards the window.

"I'm going to go out on the porch and watch, if I might."

"Sure, let me help you."

Isabella smiled. "I think if you just open the door, I'll be fine."

"I see that." But he helped her anyway.

The sky held a mixture of gray and distinctive white puffy clouds.

"Those are thunderheads," said Gabriel pointing.

Thunder rumbled and she saw a big drop of rain fall on the walkway.

"This is so amazing. So … majestic. It's like seeing the power of God, in nature."

Gabriel quietly searched the sky and then said, "That's a good way of looking at it. Animals certainly seem to understand that it is a sound to adhere to. I don't think I've ever had a dog that wasn't afraid of thunder."

He stood beside her and she gave his hand a pat. "This is a nice moment to share," she said, and Gabriel nodded.

"I've been so used to being alone, that I'd forgotten there are moments like this that are nice to be shared."

They quietly watched the sky until the wind blew rain their way, then went inside the cabin.

Gabriel didn't want to let go of her after he saw her to a chair. She looked at him, her eyes questioning, but he only gave her an exaggerated pat on her shoulder as he let go.

Bella can touch my soul with only her eyes, he thought, which was as amazing to him as the storm had been for her. She searched for answers in her own right. At least she did something about her life, however dangerous it may be. Gabriel had thought he was doing something about his life too, but now wondered if by coming out west, he was in fact unconsciously hiding from life. He rubbed his forehead at the thought, pained at the idea.

"Why do you think I came out west?" he asked.

Her eyebrows shot up in surprise. "Well, hmm. Let me think. To get away from where you were at the close of the war. I'm thinking you wanted a new life but didn't want to be swayed by your family into something you weren't ready for, so you traveled in the opposite direction."

A loud burst of thunder, startled Isabella, but to him it was an omen because he suddenly realized just what he'd done. He'd run away from all he knew. Like a dying dog, he ran off to the woods to lick his wounds. That's as far as he'd gotten.

"I think that's what you've communicated to me. Except the part about your family, I just guessed that."

"Yes, that's a pretty good assumption from what I've expressed."

"Do you know what you want now?"

"Not yet, but I'm starting to make a little progress," he said, knowing that Bella had made this 'dog' want to leave the woods for the first time. He didn't want to say anymore, so he left the cabin to grab some firewood.

THE NEXT DAY Gabriel went to work, so Isabella decided she'd make an effort to start paying him back for all he'd done for her.

With one hand, she cleaned the grime off the walls with Edgar's cleaner, while the other held onto her crutch. She was slow, but she had enough muscle to be effective. She found some vinegar and made an all-purpose cleaning solution for the rest of the cabin.

Finally, she put some soup on to boil using the leftover turkey and drippings and added vegetables from the root cellar.

To her satisfaction, she learned that with practice she fared well with one leg and the crutch. As a result, her plan was to leave for Haines next week, if at all possible.

While she hated to leave a man she'd never forget, she knew he was not ready to settle down. For that matter, neither was she - she had dreams to fulfill first. It took some doing, but she pushed all thoughts of leaving Gabriel from her mind; she had no other choice.

After a long period of reclining, she got out flour, salt, and lard, and mixed together some drop biscuits. She blew sprigs of hair from her face and smiled at the finished results.

Isabella couldn't be prouder when Gabriel came in the door. His eyes widened, then he smiled.

"I don't know which to be more thankful for, the cleaning or the cooking. Smells good, in more ways than one."

"Thank you. I'm just glad to start paying you back."

"Well, I'm glad you cooked because I'm exhausted." He flopped down in a chair. "How's your leg?"

"I feel like putting my feet up and I will shortly. Tell me about what you did today."

"Yeah, I suppose you're tired of being stuck in the cabin and could use some news from the outside."

She nodded.

"I learned there was a robbery along the Powder River, between Sumpter and Baker City." He pulled off a boot. "Easier way to get gold, I guess."

"That's awful."

He nodded. "Takes all kinds to make up the world. In my world, I worked on shoes for burros and mended wheels, mainly."

"Did you enjoy your day?"

"I know you're just making small talk now, Bella."

She shook her head. "No, I really want to know if you enjoy what you do."

"Well, I like getting the extra money. I don't like the heat unless it's a cold day." He looked down in thought. "I suppose there is the internal reward of fixing or making something."

She looked at the ceiling and sighed, feeling a little burst of joy over her future. "Yeah, well I think I will love teaching. I'm excited about getting started."

She looked back at him in time to see him frown.

"Don't worry. I'll be safe."

"I know, you have a gun."

CHAPTER 11

The following day, Gabriel sprinted up the terraces. Usually he was exhausted by the time he left his job to go home. Tonight, his adrenalin was pumping by the time he reached the cabin door.

"Welcome home, Gabriel," Isabella said with a bright smile.

He didn't answer. He didn't know what to say.

"Are you okay?" she asked.

"No. I'm upset. With you. Sit down."

With a hand to her chest, she sat down and said, "I've been here all day."

He took a chair and moved it so he could be eye to eye with her. "It's not about today."

"You're scaring me. What are you talking about?"

Like a jack-in-the-box, Gabriel stood with hands on hips. "At work today, Benjamin told me about the stage robbery."

"There was another stage robbery?" Isabella asked.

"I'm referring to the one you were involved in."

Suddenly she grew quiet and looked down at her lap, like a chastised schoolgirl.

Suddenly he felt like a father. "Don't you have anything to say about this?"

She sighed. "Nobody would have done a thing if I hadn't intervened."

His forefinger was near her nose. "You pushed him over with your foot! Do you know what could have happened to you?"

"Nothing did. Everybody got their belongings back."

He sat down, scooted his chair back and put a hand to his forehead. "You seem to think you are invincible, like danger is for other people."

She lifted her chin. "The man treated me like I was made of china or something. He put me behind him, on a log all by myself. Perhaps he thought I was going to faint any minute. Men seem to think that fainting is just a part of being a female, and I happen to differ with that fact."

"Obviously."

"Well, you're a doctor, you should differ with that fact, too."

He put his elbows on his knees and his chin in his hands. "Not every woman in the world grew up with six brothers and if they did, they may find that it was a privilege to have the protection of so many males."

"I'm sorry, but I don't roll over and play dead. I am a person with a brain, who can use it to make her way in the world."

He reached out and took her hand and said quietly. "I respect that, I really do, but intelligence needs to be mixed with common sense. You are not invincible, Bella. Part of being a young person is thinking that you are."

She let go of his hand. "Well, you haven't hit thirty either, Gabriel. You may not think you're infallible, no, quite the opposite. You have hid yourself in these woods because of what you might have to face in the world."

After a look of astonishment, he scooted his chair back and turned to the door. "I'm going to wash up outside."

"I'm sorry," she said when he came back in. She hadn't moved and her hands fidgeted with the lap of her dress. "I just - "

He held up a hand to interrupt her. "I said my peace and you said yours. Nothing more should be said."

She supposed he was right and sighed in response.

"A GENTLEMAN CALLER HERE FOR ISABELLA."

"What?" She'd been staring out the back window and had no idea they'd had company.

Someone stepped in behind Gabriel, a man dressed in a charcoal gray suit and top hat. He smiled and then presented her with his card.

"This is Lawrence Scott," introduced Gabriel.

"Uh … it's Terrence Scott."

"Oh sorry," Gabriel said with a half-smile.

Terrence took his hat in his hands. "I came to see how you are faring, Miss Moore."

"Oh, well, I'm doing fine, thank you. Won't you sit down?"

She saw Gabriel shake his head a moment too late.

Terrence sat at the edge of the wooden chair and put his elbows on his knees. His hands fiddled with his hat. "I'm glad you are doing okay. When you are able to get around town a little better, I'd like to buy you dinner at the hotel."

This time she did see Gabriel shake his head and she wondered if he knew this man. On second thought, she doubted it as he didn't even get his name right.

"I don't know, Mr. Scott. I'm not planning to stay in town for very long." She didn't say when because she didn't want to discuss it with Gabriel. Just yet.

"Oh, I'm sorry to hear this. I was hoping you'd stay."

Isabella realized suddenly that she wanted to hear these same words from Gabriel, not from Terrence or anyone else.

"I thank you again, and it was a wonderful invitation, but I'll be leaving relatively soon. I must decline."

"I understand. Where will you be going?"

"I'm going to be teaching school in Haines."

"Oh, but that is just over the hill. Surely - "

"But - " Gabriel and Isabella said at the same time.

Isabella looked at Gabriel with furrowed brow, a signal to let her continue. "Yes, Haines is not far as the crow flies, but it isn't a trip I want to make very many times, nor do I wish the stage trip on another. But thank you, anyway."

After grabbing her crutch, she stood as a signal for Terrence to leave. When he didn't move, she said, "Thank you for stopping by. Gabriel will see you out."

Isabella tried to be sweet but curt, because she didn't want anyone to interfere with the bond she'd made with Gabriel. She didn't know what the relationship was exactly, but nevertheless she wanted it to be non-inclusive.

Gabriel came in with a smile on his face. "He's a handsome man."

"You sound like my mother. He was okay."

He chuckled. "He was willing to go over the mountains to see you again."

"I should have told him I have six brothers who will skin his hide soon as they get the chance."

"Hey, wait a minute. Perhaps I should have given you a different name upon your arrival, so they won't be able to find you, uh … me."

"I'm thinking they would be happy you cared for me. The alternative is hard to imagine."

His smile vanished. "They must be worried sick about you."

"I will send them a note when I get to Haines. I told them I would notify them when I was settled. They can come see me there, if they wish."

"Worrying your family is wrong," he said with a sigh.

"Their treating me like a prisoner is wrong," she said sternly.

The silence was deafening.

"I think I'll lie down. It's been a busy day for me," Isabella said to Gabriel. And she was far too exhausted to argue about anything, much less her family.

Her leg ached and she was too tired to sleep, which was her own fault for working herself so hard.

"My leg hurts," she said, staring at the curtain between them.

"I'm sorry."

"You're a doctor and all you can say is, I'm sorry?"

"No, I have more to say, but you probably won't like it."

"I don't need your help anyway. I've been reading your books."

"Okay, you take this patient then." The lilt in his voice uplifted her.

Isabella cleared her throat. "You, Miss Moore, spent entirely too much time on your leg today. The best method of recovery is for you to limit your movements and get lots of rest."

"Smart doctor." After a moment, he said, "Bella, I'll talk with you awhile. Maybe the conversation will keep your mind off the pain. Perhaps I can bore you to sleep. But what should we talk about?"

"Well, I've been wanting to talk to you about my friend Marie."

"Does she have a particular ailment?"

"No. It's just that I have this wonderful opportunity to talk to an actual doctor who served in the war."

She heard a displeased sigh, but her curiosity inspired her, made her follow through with her questions. "Marie is a friend of mine back home and is all for women's rights."

His chuckle encouraged her as well, so she continued. "She told me about a woman named Tomkins from Virginia. Her name was Sally, I'm thinking. Anyway, she dedicated herself to cleanliness as part of the treatment for the war's wounded. Sally's hospital was known for saving lives. Marie said that more soldiers returned to the battlefield from Sally's hospital than any other hospital in the south."

The silence could be cut with a knife, and it saddened her that she couldn't talk about this subject she'd discussed so many times with Marie. She wanted to know the truth of it.

"Hmmm," he finally said. "This Sally person had one hell-of-a job because many doctors took pride in looking like a butcher, with clothes bloodied from patients."

"Did you?" she asked and then wanted to take the words back as soon as they came out of her mouth.

"Sometimes there were so many patients that I *had* to have blood on me for a time, but I never, *never* took pride in it. Couldn't understand how anyone could. It's life blood, for goodness sake."

"I like how you think," she said and could imagine an almost smile on his face at her words.

"What did this Sally do, according to Marie?"

"My understanding is that she cleaned and washed everything, from surfaces to tools."

"Do you know what she cleaned with?"

"No, but - " She sat and leaned over to flip through books and periodicals, hoping she could see what she was looking for in the dimness of the night. "I saw an article in a more recent periodical that you had stacked with your books, perhaps you saw it? It has to do with just this line of thinking."

Isabella stopped her rustling when she heard Gabriel moving about. It sounded like he decided to get dressed. She put a hand on her mouth fearing she'd upset him enough to make him leave the cabin.

CHAPTER 12

Gabriel lit a lantern and walked to her side of the room divider.

"Can you find it?" he asked.

Her eyes went to his chest, to the fine hairs that sprinkled his chest and tapered down to a point at the waistband of his pants. "What?"

He gave her a concerned look. "The paper you were just talking about."

She leaned over and grasped the periodical. "I'll try to sum it up. There is a doctor named Lister that heard that carbolic acid was used to treat sewage in the fields. The acid killed parasites that cause disease, and so the cattle eating from this field didn't get sick.

"Lister also noticed that there was a difference between a broken bone like mine and a broken bone that protruded from the skin and reached the air. Lister made a connection to what he learned about the treated sewage to broken bones. The leg with a broken bone that reached the air was far more likely to be amputated than those with a break like mine. He said that there is bacteria in the air that gets into an unclean wound causing decay. He wanted to destroy the bacteria that entered the wound. So, he's been using the carbolic acid on wounds such as these with some success. Do you see the connection, Gabriel?"

"I'm not sure what you mean."

"The connection between Sally's keeping things clean and Lister taking it a step further by keeping wounds clean, too?"

"Can I see the article?"

"Of course, it is yours." She handed it to him, and he returned to his side of the room.

Isabella lay back down and looked at the ceiling, at the shadows made by the lantern. She was pretty sure the periodicals he'd pushed into the bookcase hadn't been read. It was part of his putting it all aside to focus on a new career. Yet, if she was not mistaken, he'd found it just as interesting as she did, otherwise he wouldn't have taken the article to read himself.

"OHH!" Isabella put a hand to her mouth. It sounded like someone was trying to knock the door of the cabin down. Her wide eyes watched Gabriel move to the door.

A gray-bearded man pushed the door open, causing Gabriel to back up for safety.

"Doc! Doc! There's been a cave in. We've lost three men, but we got my brother Charlie out. He's hurt bad. Will you help?"

Obviously, the town knew that Gabriel took on emergencies, because the man didn't wait for consent. Four men carried Charlie in. At the table, Gabriel took a newspaper, and a few medical books Isabella had been skimming through, and set them aside.

Isabella put a hand over her mouth. Charlie was covered

in blood and dust giving him a gray hue which couldn't be more disturbing as it made him look dead. If it wasn't for the other dust covered miners she probably would have screamed.

"Things like this happen in the mines," Gabriel told her. "They all know it; they take a chance. You can move to the edge of the room or you can go outside, it's up to you."

"Just a minute," he said to the men holding Charlie. He washed his hands and went over a blacksmith's hard to clean nails with a brush. He fit an old, but clean, white sheet on the table.

While they settled Charlie on the table, he focused on getting some tools from a bag, then grabbed a bottle of vodka from a cupboard.

Isabella knew she should do something but didn't know what to do. Having studied a fair share of medical books gave her an interest in Charlie. Yet, she knew with a lack of mobility, she'd end up getting in the way. She stepped back into the farthest corner of the room as Gabriel suggested, and shot up a quick prayer to God.

Gabriel told the men to step back. He took a wet cloth and wiped it over Charlie, looking for the extent of his injuries. To no one in particular he said, "It's not surprising he's unconscious; he took a pretty nasty blow to the head."

With a pair of shears, he cut off Charlie's torn shirt. "His breathing is labored, probably at least broken ribs. I see blood on his pants. I'll have to get them off." One boot fell and then the other. He took another sheet and partially covered him so that his privates were hidden when his pants came off.

Charlie's leg was broken in two places. A bone protruded from his lower leg. Gabriel exchanged glances with Isabella, both knowing what that could mean.

"Will his leg have to come off?" asked his brother, hat in hand.

"I'll do all I can to save it." Apparently, the man believed he could as he let out a breath of relief.

"I'm a little concerned about his head." He wiped at the blood on his head again. The men looked down at the floor in unison, and he so wanted to say he would be okay.

"I want to keep Charlie here tonight. You boys go on. Come back by in the morning. Right now, Isabella and I will make a cast of sorts to help his leg heal properly. I'll also tape his ribs."

Isabella would help, she would, but she wondered at the same time why he didn't ask someone else.

"Why me?" she asked when the others left.

"You've been reading my medical books," he said with a smile. "In actuality, Charlie doesn't need a room full of visitors, and I feel comfortable here with you."

"Well, I've stared so much at my cast, I'm sure I can help duplicate it."

"Besides, Charlie will be much happier waking up to your face instead of a bunch of old stinky miners."

She admired Gabriel's strength in emergencies. "You are as calm as can be and I am shaking like a leaf. How can that be?"

"You know I've seen my share of emergencies, but still, if I'm too frazzled then I'm in the wrong business."

She wondered if he realized what he said, as she washed her hands.

He'd been getting something out of the supply closet. It looked like some sort of tape. She made it to Charlie's side to help with his ribs. Feeling awkward, she stood wringing her hands.

"Start by talking softly to Charlie."

"But he's unconscious."

"I believe in talking to my patients in the event that he or she can hear me at some point.

"Charlie, you don't look so good."

"Try something a little more positive. Now, I'm going to put him on his side. When I lift him, put the fabric down."

Isabella pushed at the fabric as quickly as she could but felt like she was all thumbs.

"You don't have to hurry. Remember my arms are strong; I'm a blacksmith," he said, trying to reassure her.

"Yes." She nervously nodded and looked down at Charlie. "You are going to be all right."

"Okay, now say it normally, not with such a high pitch."

Well, at least she'd made Gabriel smile. "Charlie, you're going to be all right."

"That sounded almost believable." He lifted Charlie again and she placed the tape under him.

"Wait until you see this angel who is helping you. You can open your eyes anytime and take a look," he said.

"Will he ... ?"

"We should know more by tomorrow," he told her quietly.

"Okay, Charlie, I'm planning to have breakfast with you in the morning."

"Thank you, Bella."

Gabriel prepared to put a cast on Charlie's leg. "Did you wonder what the vodka was for?"

"I thought it was for Charlie in the event he woke up."

"Vodka is the closest thing I have to the carbolic acid that Lister talked about in the article. Actually, alcohols are similar to the acid, but really must be oxidized, but I can't do that. Yet. So here goes."

"Hope is springing eternal here," she said with a big smile. "I will continue to pray."

~

"Hi, Charlie. My name is Isabella. I've been helping nurse you along."

He focused on her briefly, then winced and closed his eyes. She knew it would be better to let him sleep, but at the same time she wanted to know how he fared cognitively.

At present, she couldn't ask Gabriel what she should do as he'd left early to hunt for fresh meat. He thought Charlie would be under for a while longer and that this was his best opportunity to be out.

She knew only a fraction of the pain Charlie felt in comparison to her accident, so she let him sleep.

Deep inside somewhere a longing to help him rose. In assessing the whole situation, he didn't look comfortable to her. Somehow, he'd moved during the night and she longed to straighten him out and clean the smudges of dirt they'd missed the first time around. As best she could with one good leg, she put her arms under his shoulders and pulled him toward her, then hopped to the end of the table and straightened his legs.

She knew from discussions with Gabriel that it was possible he could lose his leg, as the bone was exposed to the air. She hoped and then prayed that Lister's theory was right and that pouring the vodka on the wound had killed the bacteria so that his leg could be saved. Besides the life changing event of losing a leg for Charlie, she feared that Gabriel would be even less enamored with being a doctor. From what she'd seen, Gabriel was a fine doctor and found it hard to think of him giving it up to become a blacksmith.

CHAPTER 13

The door opened and Gabriel backed in with a skinned rabbit. "Good morning."

"Good morning," she answered with an expanding heart. Inside she felt like a hound dog, excited to see his master, every time he came back to the cabin.

He looked over at Charlie before he said, "I snared a rabbit as you can see. I also found one of those wood rats in one of my traps, so yes we have rats around here."

She frowned. "Well, I prefer to think about the rabbit we'll eat instead. By the way, Charlie woke briefly, looked at me than went back to sleep."

He smiled from ear-to-ear, which told her that first and foremost he was a doctor, no matter what he said. "That's a good sign, Bella."

Gabriel took time to show Isabella pulse points on Charlie. "The idea is to count beats per minute. Charlie's pulse is weak as you can tell."

She shook her head.

"Here, check the pulse in my neck, then check Charlie's."

Isabella slowly, attentively, reached up to touch him. She

knew he wanted to keep space between them, so she was caught off guard. Her breath left her when their eyes connected, and he took her hand and placed it under his ear. She lowered her gaze, then closed her eyes so that she could focus.

"I feel it," she said.

"Now try Charlie."

It startled her at first because she couldn't feel a pulse, but when she did, she looked back to Gabriel in concern.

"I see you can tell the difference between a strong beating heart and someone who's been through some trauma."

"Yes, your heart is much stronger and faster."

"The fast part comes from standing so close to a beautiful woman."

She smiled.

"Believe me, Charlie will appreciate waking to a woman."

"I hope I can help him in some way."

He studied her face for a moment. "Are you interested in minding the bandages?"

"I do want to help him. Yes."

"Tomorrow we'll check the bandages together. I'll show you what to look for."

She nodded.

That night, she woke often to listen to Charlie's shallow breathing, fearing he wouldn't make it. Not only did she not want this man to die, she wanted to see the vodka do its work on Charlie's leg.

Honestly, it was Gabriel's interest in medicine that made her want to learn more, to pick up the periodicals to find information about the human body and wholeness.

The new research taking place can save life and limb. It was awe-inspiring to think about, and phenomenal to be part of trying to put this research to use. Her life would never be the same again.

~

"HE'S A GOOD DOCTOR, ain't he?" asked Charlie.

"Yes," said Isabella, looking up from a periodical.

"Each day that passes, I think I'm going to keep my leg."

She nodded. "Thankfully it appears that way." She was also glad that he had only a little brain damage. According to Charlie's brother, he was slower to answer, but he did appear to comprehend.

After a moment of silence, she added. "It seems the war has taken a lot from Gabriel. It has festered itself inside him like a wound that won't heal, I'm afraid."

"I believe he's grievin' still," Charlie said matter-of-factly.

"Grieving?" She'd never thought of that.

"I lost my daughter years ago. She wanted to go hunting with me one day. I told her no, but she followed me anyways. She snuck out of the house before her mama knew. My wife thought I'd let her go with me. She was but seven years old … "

He was silent for a moment and she put a hand on his. "I'm sorry, Charlie."

He looked at her absently. "Seems she took a fall from an outcrop of rock and hit her head just so."

Isabella sucked in a breath through her teeth. "Oh, Charlie."

"I see the same look in Doc's face. He was helpless to do anything about the situation he was put in, and yet he was supposed to, being in charge and all."

She couldn't argue with that.

"He cared about those people, and I cared about my daughter. He's grievin', is what he's doing."

"Does the grieving last for a lifetime, Charlie?"

He shook his head. "Time heals all wounds, they say.

Grievin' comes on you when you least expect it at times, but as time passes by, it hits you less and less often."

She sighed, then said, "I think Gabriel thinks being a blacksmith is the career for him, and will one day stop practicing completely."

"Perhaps it's 'cause being a doc is a constant reminder."

"It would seem so."

CHAPTER 14

"Panning doesn't cost much to get started, maybe a shovel, bucket and a pan," said Gabriel. "A pick would help, and a little bit of mercury, but mostly you need a huge amount of patience and energy to keep at it. Plus, practice makes perfect."

Isabella nodded excitedly. She had that, yes, she had patience.

"You'll be looking for gold that has washed down from the mountains and settled in creek beds."

"Do you just dip anywhere in the creek?"

"Good question, Bella. No, you need to look where the current has ebbed or in a sandy area."

"Will I find nuggets?"

"Or flakes. I don't want you to get your hopes up too high."

He helped her out the door and moved her off the porch to behind the cabin.

"What's this?"

"This is going to be a safe place to pan for gold. I managed to get a bucket of dirt from a friend's claim and water from the spring behind the cabin."

"What do you mean by safe place? Why can't I go to the creek like everyone else? I thought it would be fun to go down there."

Gabriel put his hands on his hips. "Do you want to make a scene? Do you want several miners breathing down your neck trying to help you? Or, maybe you'd prefer to watch a fight over you?"

She frowned. "That wouldn't really happen would it?"

"I don't want to find out, I have to protect my hands, you know."

His words sent her spiraling from joyfulness to irritation. She wanted to address why he wanted to keep his hands free from injury, to be a doctor or a blacksmith? She supposed it didn't really matter anyway.

Isabella only wanted to be at the creek to enjoy the ambiance. Now she felt sorry for herself, but then shook her head as if to clear it, trying desperately to appreciate what she had right here. She'd wanted to learn how to pan, and even though the setting wasn't as she'd imagined it, it was happening right now.

However, a sigh did escape. To cover her frustration, she said, "Well, as long as you're not hiding me because you're ashamed of me."

He took his hands from his hips. "No, that's not it at all."

Gabriel helped her to a tree stump and put dirt and water in her pan.

Immediately her spirits lifted. "Oh, I see some gold!"

"No, you see pyrite. Fool's Gold. You can shatter iron pyrite but not gold. The gold is heavy and will drop to the bottom. You'll soon be able to see the difference."

. . .

Gabriel looked around. He didn't think he'd have to deal with neighbors this morning since most were off mining. Yet he was pretty sure someone would sniff out Isabella and come running. Sure enough, his neighbor Thomas headed their way.

"Nice weather we're having," Thomas said and Gabriel looked up at the cloudy sky.

"Hello, Miss. Are you feeling better today?"

"Yes, I am. Thank you very much."

Thomas stood and watched them for a moment, or more aptly watched Isabella. He didn't even try to hide his boldness but sat down on a rock and propped his head on his hand.

Isabella intently watched Gabriel get her started and often met his eyes with a smile. Her smile almost made him forget what he was doing; however, having an observer helped him focus on the work at hand.

In no time, neighbor Paul, from just down the terrace, joined Thomas on an outcropping of rock. Paul commented on the weather as well.

"Would you like me to help, ma'am?" asked Paul.

"No, thank you. I learn by doing and I really want to learn how to do this by myself."

"Did you hear that Thomas? She learns by doing."

Gabriel was not sure if Paul meant to make an off-color remark, but he took no chances.

"We could use some help with Charlie inside. If you wish to help, that is."

The two men gasped in unison. "You mean doctoring?" asked Thomas.

"No, more like nursing."

They both stood instantly and brushed off the seat of their pants. While turning to leave, Paul said, "Time to get to work myself. I'm running late this morning."

Isabella chuckled when they cleared earshot. Her laughter floated across his senses like a bird flitting through a beautiful blue sky.

Gabriel tried to tell himself her twinkling eyes were due to her finally being able to pan for gold. Once he'd convinced himself, he walked back to the cabin to check on Charlie and maintain a grip on himself.

From start to finish, she'd made it through a five-pound bucket of dirt. She found flakes, but no nuggets. Gabriel wished now he would have salted it with a nugget.

Nevertheless, Isabella's exuberance through the whole thing reminded him of a child at Christmas, ready to open presents. She overflowed with happiness over something as simple as learning something new. Something she'd only dreamed of. The happiness was contagious as well.

Her twinkling emerald eyes coupled with her enthusiasm sucked him in. Made him want to come out of his moodiness and move back to the land of the living.

He couldn't help but stare out the window at her and wonder if she was only a dream. A dream he never wanted to wake from. It suddenly struck him that this sunny sky she brought with her would be dark again when she moved on to Haines. He had to turn from the window now, so that he could process this information without her in sight.

But before he could weigh his thoughts, Isabella called him to the cabin door. "What?"

"Come out here." Her teasing smile made him skeptical.

Gabriel still couldn't take his eyes off Isabella. At first it was because she was his patient. Next, he told himself that it was because women were scarce in these parts. The truth of it was she not only brought color to his life, but tenderness to his soul, and a smile to his hardened face.

By the time he came to Cracker City, he didn't care if he'd ever see a woman again. Sometime during the war, he'd forgotten about the need she'd stirred in the core of his body. Every day now, he thought of the physical ramifications and being near her filled his head with possibilities. Yet, when he wasn't looking at her, he knew he didn't have anything to offer her. He had no sure employment, other than in this mining town, that he could tell her father about.

And damn her, she knew the facts as well, but egged him on anyway. She couldn't be naïve enough to not know she affected him physically, could she? Perhaps. He guessed he'd have to ask her to be sure, and here was an opportunity.

At the door, Isabella pretended to lose her balance and threw her arms around the middle of his waist. He believed it wasn't an accident because after she entwined herself the crutch fell to the ground. Her arms wrapped around him so tightly that he couldn't loosen them as he turned toward her.

He looked down into a smile so big that he could see both sets of even white teeth. How could he not return this smile?

"Did you lose your balance, Bella?"

"You know, I still like how you say my name."

He raised an eyebrow in question. "Did you lose your balance?"

"Um … no."

It was almost funny the way her arms moved to his neck and he smiled because of it. "What are you doing then? Are you only appreciating what I've done for you?"

"Certainly."

Darn her, she stared at his lips waiting for him to kiss her. He had two choices; he could push her away or wait her out and put things in her hands.

Instead their eyes connected, and he felt an almost electric pull from his eyes down to the core of his belly. Automatically, he tightened her already firm grip and took her lips gently. She touched her tongue to his lips, and he savored it with the intention of chastising her for wrapping herself around him at any moment.

At any moment.

Just a moment more.

Finally, he pulled her head back and looked at her dazzled eyes. "Why are you doing this?"

"Because I like it?" she answered in the form of a question.

"Bella."

She sighed, satisfied, when he said her name once again. "My friend Marie says that there is nothing wrong with a woman making a move."

"You can't just grab a man and start kissing him."

A frown marred her pretty face. "Why not? I would like to talk to anyone who says I can't."

"Perhaps you're getting some practice in, until the right man comes along. Hmm?"

"What? That's crazy."

He supposed he liked hearing that answer, but he had to be the responsible one here. "I don't think you realize what happens to a man when kissed, so - "

"Tell me what happens, Gabriel," she said with a lilt in her voice.

"Come on. You can't be eighteen and not know what happens to a man's body."

Her bottom lip protruded. "I'm twenty-one."

"Then you should already know."

"How does it make *you* feel?"

There goes that smile again. He closed his eyes and said it. "I feel lust for you."

"You do?" she asked in a rising voice, which made him lust even more. Lust mixed with frustration now.

"Why do you pull this out of me?" He almost added "Bella," but thought better of it.

"I enjoy kissing you. I really enjoy kissing you."

"Well, I suppose I feel complimented, but you know what this could lead to, don't you?"

"Uh ... yes."

She kept one hand on his arm and reached down for her crutch. After propping it under her arm, she said, "Why is it that it's okay for a man to kiss, or whatever he wants to do, but a woman can't? It hardly seems fair, don't you think?"

"I think you better not have this conversation with another man, because he will try to take advantage of you."

"And you won't?" Her question held a tone of defeat.

"I'm trying hard to treat you with respect."

"So, you won't respect me if I stay in your arms too long?"

It was like dangling a steak in front of a hungry dog. He put a hand across his face.

"Why me, Isabella? Is it because I'm available?"

"No. I'm infatuated with you."

Suddenly fear gripped him in his gut, and he shook his head. He wasn't ready for this. "You're a beautiful woman and you can have any man you want. You need to look for someone who is ready to marry you."

She turned from Gabriel, speechless.

"Good, I see you understand what I'm trying to say."

Isabella nodded.

He sighed. He didn't want to hurt her, only wanted her to think realistically. Yet, realistically, he only wanted her more now. Her words of praise and attraction went straight to his head and lingered. Now that he knew she wanted him, he couldn't even let her touch him. Although he longed for her too, he'd have to keep her at arm's length.

He didn't mean to make her cry. How he hated a woman's tears.

CHAPTER 15

Isabella thought her broken leg was painful, but the wound Gabriel inflicted held advantage. A weight of some kind pressed down in the area of her heart making her want to be alone to cry. Still, even though she wasn't alone, she went to bed, put the covers over her, and cried as quietly as she could into the pillow.

Besides Gabriel's handsomeness, he was a good and kind man, and far more in control than her. Whether he cared for her at all, she didn't know, but he protected her as if he did. Yet how did he even know what she wanted from him as she didn't even know herself, however, she did know that he was the first man she'd ever really wanted to kiss.

When she got home, she had a thing or two to say to Marie about making a move on a man.

She considered her suitors at home. Every last one of them seemed eager to kiss her. She had to take the initiative with Gabriel and would have even if Marie hadn't suggested a woman's right to make the first move. Perhaps her infatuation had to do with Gabriel's reserve toward her.

Who was she kidding? She cared about Gabriel for many reasons. He was worthy of her love.

Her tears dried when she realized that one of the things she liked most about him was that he didn't even suggest that she stop pursuing her dreams. True, he wanted her to have a chaperone, but that would be the only drawback.

She wondered if there could ever be a time for them in the future. Her mother always said, if it was meant to be it would happen.

Because she was down, she thought about home. Soon her mother and father would be finishing off the fall work and be ready to head into the winter months.

ISABELLA'S WORDS came to mind. "My friend Marie says that there is nothing wrong with a woman making a move."

Isabella was sweet, but wild at heart, taking chances, not taking anything too serious. Gabriel didn't even remember the last time he'd felt carefree and he envied her entrance into this often-cruel world.

She humored him like nothing else had in a long time. She tried to make him smile, and it felt good that someone cared enough to try.

But the flirting was not okay, too careless for a young lady passing through. Especially from a woman who says she's not interested in getting married, only finding a job. How can this be right in her eyes? he wondered.

He rubbed his face. Ideally, the smarter thing to do would be to talk this out first, come to a complete understanding without tears. He was only a man, not a saint, with feelings and desires like any other man. Perhaps he should take advantage of her innocence and make her his. If she didn't stop his advances, he'd put his mark on her forever. Yet, he knew the thought was frivolous. It would be wrong to take advantage of her naiveté, to try and bind him to her as she had more to do before settling down, and he had more to do before settling up.

As it was, this man had nothing to offer besides a few gold nuggets of which she'd really like to find on her own anyway. What she needed from him was a caretaker, a doctor to fix her until she was off doing her bidding or living her friend Marie's dreams.

GABRIEL'S WORDS were merely a warning, a reality check for her and, she supposed, wisdom she needed to grasp at her young age. As Gabriel suggested, she was lucky he hadn't taken advantage of her.

Was it wrong to want him? she wondered. Must be because she felt chastised for needing him. However, she'd been stupid to think that they should have a courtship, as she'd inwardly set limitations to their relationship.

She would move on without him, and then what? Come back here? What could she do here? Gabriel to Haines? What would he do there, where a blacksmith wasn't as needed? Besides, she wanted to go home after her job was over anyway.

Yes, she'd been foolish, thinking only of the moment and the giddiness she felt when in Gabriel's arms. He intoxicated her so much that she only thought in the present. Further, he made no mention of any plans to marry in his future, let alone at this time.

Did she really want a man who'd lost God somewhere, where her God was ever present to her - except when in Gabriel's arms? At first it was a fun game, but then she lost sight of everything important. Oh goodness, how weak she turned out to be when she should have been her strongest! Sure, it hurt to be rejected, but it also hurt to learn your principles were compromised as well.

With an exhale, she decided that she would not act foolishly with Gabriel again, she'd regain her pride by not only keeping her hands to herself, but by living up to her standards in the few days she had left in Cracker City.

FROM THE DOORWAY, Gabriel could see Isabella's elbow and part of her long hair at the edge of the blanket dividing the room. Silky red hair moved back and forth with the rhythm of the hairbrush. She didn't see him, so he stole a minute to gaze at her beauty. He wanted to go to her now, to touch her hair, her face and body.

She'd be leaving here soon, he knew, as he'd seen good progress on a daily basis. Even someone without medical training could see that. He also knew that she'd take the brightness from this cabin and the light she brought to his dark life. She probably didn't even know she created that light for him.

He turned to look at Charlie, the man who kept him from going to her at this moment. Charlie dozed, unaffected by their morning routine.

Soon Charlie'd be on his way, too. With both legs. He'd made a difference this time, with the help of the articles Isabella told him about. He'd almost hoped there'd be another mine accident so that he could see if this new procedure, the killing of bacteria, was luck or if Lister's theory made sense. After shaking his head at his foolishness for thinking this way about another human being, he headed outside to check traps.

~

As the cabin door closed, Isabella set her brush down and pushed back the blanket as she would a curtain. She caught sight of Charlie, now stirring.

"Good morning, Charlie."

"Good morning, Isabella."

She grabbed her crutch and limped over to him. "Feeling okay?"

He nodded, watching her near him. "I've been praying. Nothing makes a person more religious than being hurt."

"I suppose there is some truth to your statement. We tend to take for granted our good health until we get sick or injured."

"Yep. Not only have I prayed for healing, but I've been praying just to say thanks, too. I know how blessed I am to be in such good shape today."

"Seems like we just get busy and forget to do that, but counting our blessings can only make us happier," she added with a smile.

"Hey, Gabriel seemed to have stepped out for a moment. I suppose if I tried to help you to the outhouse, we wouldn't get very far."

"I can wait a bit."

Some minutes later, Gabriel returned. "Nothing in the traps this morning," he said, looking toward Charlie.

"Can't win 'em all," Charlie replied.

Isabella caught Gabriel's eye. "How about I make some biscuits while you help Charlie out?"

"Sounds grand to me," said Charlie and both men smiled.

Gabriel stepped back in the cabin about the time Isabella prepared to roll out the dough. "Charlie's out on the porch, taking in some fresh air," he said and stepped behind her. With one hand he moved the strands of hair that had fallen from her top knot and put his lips against the back of her neck.

She wanted to ask what had gotten into him, or turn around and kiss his lips, but she didn't. She put her hands in the dough and pressed hard so that it squished out between her fingers. Instead, she closed her eyes and let it happen, then stepped to the side.

Three times she'd tried to get him to give her this type of attention, and he didn't go for it for good reasons. She'd been playing with fire, acting selfishly and wantonly, against everything she'd been taught and believed. She knew she was leaving shortly and not only that, after three refusals she couldn't stand the heartbreak of another. Besides it hurt so much, it frightened her to think of it happening again.

All of a sudden they'd both changed and she dare not ask about his change of heart as she knew he could easily persuade her to do something she shouldn't.

"Bella?"

The way he said her name took all of her effort to not turn into his arms. Instead she stiffened and shook her head no.

After a moment of silence, he walked out to see Charlie. She looked down and focused on the dough, punching and kneading it for all she was worth.

Bella looked so right in his kitchen, humming and making biscuits. In such a short time she'd managed to wedge into his life, and now nothing was ever going to be the same again.

She looked so beautiful, so colorful with her red hair and emerald eyes, contrasting with her ivory skin. The length of her neck especially caught his attention and he pushed away all sober thought as he neared and put his lips on the nap of her neck.

Thank goodness she was strong and refused him, yet now he knew the sting of rejection, from someone he cared for very much. He supposed payback was rightly his.

He'd thought he was so strong, and he was strong, until now. But she'd given him so much attention, that he could think of nothing else now but her lips on his. The knowledge that she wanted him was like putting alcohol on fire, a fiery combustion. Further, he felt her melting into his kiss before she thought better of it, stiffened and moved aside.

Lord help him, because he didn't think he could survive her flirting again.

CHAPTER 16

Isabella couldn't sleep due to the noisy rat, or whatever it was. Apparently, the rat liked the underside of the cabin on her half the best. More precisely, it sounded like the noise came from right under the window. She hoped it was an animal and not a man, anyway, and decided to look underneath the edge of the cabin in the morning.

When Gabriel left for work, she took a stubby candle and maneuvered herself and her cast in such a way that she could see a small pile of debris. She poked a small branch at it and a rat ran out not one foot from her. They both let out a shriek.

Now she knew what the problem was, a furry, not-so-little, rat, the same kind that intruded on her own family a few years ago. She ran the candle as close as she could to the nest looking for babies but didn't see any. Something bright and shiny caught her eye and she stuck her head in closer. Reaching out as far as she could, she picked up a small yellow rock. She saw another and took it as well.

After scooting back, she opened her hand to the sunlight

and found she had two gold nuggets. She'd heard pack rats liked shiny objects, and here in her hand was the proof.

THE CABIN DOOR OPENED, and Gabriel walked in and set his lunch box near the sink. After washing his hands and face in a bowl of water, he turned toward Isabella and Charlie. They both sat on Charlie's makeshift bed mere feet from his, with their heads bent over a game of checkers.

"Gotcha!" said Charlie.

"You're just too good for me, old man," she said fondly and smiled at Gabriel as he neared them.

"Good day?" she asked.

Her smile went from ear to ear and her exuberance made him want to answer that he'd thought of her every minute of the day. "Workday went fine. Busy."

"Anybody striking it rich?" asked Charlie.

"Donald Dowling found some good-sized nuggets. Wants to sell his mine now."

"Oh, he did? Can't wait to get back out there."

"In no time, you'll be able to do some panning if nothing else."

Charlie nodded.

"Why don't you play the next game, Gabriel? I will get something together for supper."

"Sounds like a mighty fine trade."

In passing, her hand brushed his and his senses lit up like a stack of dry kindling. Their eyes met and held until he sucked in a breath and slowly turned toward the game board.

Gabriel half watched her as she prepared a bean dish. She'd be gone soon as she could manage well enough with a crutch. Her job would begin shortly, and she'd not miss her opportunity. Still, he hoped she'd stay long enough to help with Charlie and thought maybe she would since she'd not mentioned leaving for a time.

And what would he say when she finally did bring up the subject? He supposed it didn't matter because she had no reason to stay and every reason to go. However, they did need to discuss how she could travel safely to Haines. At least he could help her with that.

As Isabella changed Charlie's bed sheet, she decided it was time to go. If she could tend to Charlie, she could manage by herself nearly anywhere.

Charlie started to move around, taking steps or hopping across the room. No doubt, it was time for him to go back to his brother's care anyway.

She hadn't told Gabriel she wanted to leave, because she knew he wouldn't let her go alone. She understood his reasons since the last stage she was on had a robbery, a wreck, and two were killed. Yet, she didn't want to be responsible for putting someone else in danger either. But she'd be fine, she knew. No one she grew up with in Prairie City would ever bother her due to her courage and vivacity, and there was a reason for that, she reminded herself.

Gabriel left for the blacksmith's shop about thirty minutes ago and Charlie lay sleeping. On her side of the room she took a sponge bath, dressed to travel and packed her bag.

The stage was due to come through Cracker City in about an hour. She took a note for Gabriel, with the two gold nuggets she'd found for her care and slipped them in his bedding. In her opinion, she owed him far more than that for not leaving her to fend for herself.

She touched Charlie's shoulder and his eyes opened. "Hi, Charlie."

"You don't know what a pleasure it's been to wake up to your beautiful face. The doc's a lucky man."

She figured she'd woken him from a deep sleep because his comment didn't make sense.

He closed his eyes again. After a moment, she said, "Charlie, are you awake?"

He turned his shoulder so that he got a better look at her. "Yep. What's the matter?"

"I'm about to leave for Haines, Charlie, and I want to say good-bye."

"What?"

"Remember I told you I have a teaching job there?"

He nodded.

"You will be okay without me here today. I have some food ready for you. You'll be fine until Gabriel gets home."

He nodded again and swallowed. "I'm sad to see you go."

She smiled. "I'm sad to leave, but I have a job to attend to."

"Gabriel - "

She stopped his words by giving him a kiss on the forehead. "Good-bye, Charlie."

As she took one last look at the cabin, she shut the door and her eyes filled with tears. It broke her heart to leave Gabriel, but she knew she had to. She had dreams to fulfill and Gabriel had things to work through in his life that had nothing to do with her.

CHAPTER 17

Isabella waited for the stage on a bench against a building. She tried to shrink herself by pulling her limbs in so no one would notice her waiting there. Finally, she chuckled at herself for thinking she could hide her cumbersome cast.

Someone left Brown's paper on the bench, the newspaper that invented stories to swindle people into buying worthless mines. She hid her face behind it and as if she had a hearing impairment, ignored the men that greeted her. Though thankful for having something to keep her eyes on, she'd like to kick Brown's behind with her good foot for being such a crook.

Isabella looked up from her newspaper. Someone shouted and people started running. Someone was in danger, but she knew that Charlie and Gabriel were safe.

As she moved the paper enough to check her timepiece, she noticed a man coming toward her from the direction of the trouble. Forgetting her need to be incognito, she called after him.

"What happened?" she asked.

"A mine accident. The Irishman is hurt pretty bad."

"Thank you," she said and brought the paper back to her face.

With all of her being she wanted to run to Gabriel to see how she could help. What did the Irishman need? Does he have broken limbs? Did Gabriel need her to help him dress the wounds or apply a cast?

The stage was nearby; she could hear the rumble of the mules and the stage behind them. Indecisive, she stood up, sat down, and stood again.

Who was she kidding, Gabriel didn't really need her, he could manage on his own. He had before he met her, and he could now. Even though she wanted to help, she needed to remember that she had a job, one that she'd dreamed of for what seemed like forever. No, she needed to move on.

This time Isabella took a seat on the opposite side of the stagecoach. Not that she counted on a wreck, but wanted to be prepared, nonetheless. Only moments before the stage left, two more men climbed in. One was Terrence who'd called on her and the other was Kirkwood. She thought Kirkwood'd be in jail for attempted robbery but was apparently wrong. She turned from him to smile a greeting at Terrence.

She sighed when she saw the driver climb to the top of the stage. Micah. She repositioned her leg with the cast and hung on to her crutch to further steady herself. As she suspected, they were off and running as soon as he'd lighted.

"Where is Isabella?" Gabriel asked as he stormed into the cabin.

"She's gone," Charlie said. "Left on the stage."

"Wh … aaat?" Gabriel needed to sit down and cry because

he wanted to keep Bella. Even though his heart sank, he had no time to think about her now.

Men followed Gabriel in, and placed the patient on the table. He went to the cupboard and took out supplies, including a bottle of vodka he touched reverently, then pressed to his breast with a silent prayer.

When things calmed down the next day, Gabriel decided to write to Bella's parents. He imagined Bella would have lifted her chin at him for it, but he couldn't live with himself if something happened to her and he could have prevented it, even if only in a small way.

WHILE OTHERS MADE SMALL TALK, Isabella kept her eyes on the scenery out the window. Partly to discourage others, as Gabriel would have wanted, and partly because she wanted to memorize the area where she'd met Gabriel. Not to mention the chance she'd had to pan for gold.

At the mountain top, they all got out so that the stage could be anchored to drill steels in an effort to get them over the tip. She walked away from the others to look back over Cracker City and the area around it. Terrence walked over to her side.

"I'd like to make you an offer that I'm hoping you will find agreeable. I wanted to talk to you when you were with the doctor, but it didn't work out that way."

"Oh?" She noticed he didn't take off his hat when he'd addressed her as was the custom to do. Despite this lack of propriety, her interest was piqued. She couldn't imagine what his offer could be. A nanny perhaps?

"I would like to open a house for business in the mining district, and I want a beautiful woman, such as yourself, to run it."

She hadn't thought about running a boarding house, probably because men ran them.

"Well, I suppose I could run a boarding house, but I am planning to teach school."

"I'm sure I can triple any amount you can make as a teacher."

Kirkwood walked up beside him, and when Terrence didn't tell him to leave, she grew suspicious.

"I thank you for your kind offer, but as I said - "

"You don't seem to understand what kind of money you could make out here, ma'am."

"I'm not interested in running a boarding house, Terrence."

Kirkwood laughed then. "A boarding house? He's talking about you being a rich Madame, ma'am."

CHAPTER 18

Isabella wanted to slap Kirkwood silly, but instead backed away as best she could with a crutch. She started to fall but Terrence took her arm just in time.

"Why would you think such a thing?" she asked, aghast.

"The signs are all there, a woman traveling alone through a mining district. Twice. Only a woman of ill repute would do that."

"Show some respect," she said through clenched teeth.

"Respect? How was it living with the good doctor?"

Boy, did she want to kick him for that comment. "I was a patient, which is none of your business anyway."

Kirkwood gave her a leering grin. "What makes you think we won't take you anyway? There's two of us and only one of you."

With every ounce of being, she forced a bravado that she was far from feeling. "There are plenty of others on this stage who can help me. Step away from me or I'll scream."

"As you like," Kirkwood said bitterly and gave a mocking bow.

Isabella clasped her hands together to try and mask their shaking and moved slowly back to the waiting stage.

For the remainder of the trip, she sat with chin up. In her peripheral vision, she could see both men staring at her. She was not a fool and knew they could grab her and force her to do as they bid. Would they follow her to her new home and take her when she least expected it? Nervous sweat started to form on her forehead and upper lip.

Yet, she had options, didn't she? With two guns on her person, she thought so. But, Gabriel's voice came clearly into her mind saying, "A gun can cause you to lose your life … What do you plan to do, wave your gun around, or actually shoot to kill? Can you actually kill someone, Bella?"

Maybe she couldn't shoot someone, but she could certainly hit someone over the head with the butt of the gun.

If she lived through this, she'd tell Marie a thing or two. No matter what she said, this world happens to be a man's world. Gabriel tried to tell her that.

It was far past time to write to her family, in more ways than one.

Olina sat looking at a picture of her daughter. She then laid it down with other photographs of her children in order of their birth. She was the sixth born out of her seven children, the only girl and the only redhead amongst the brood. They named her Isabella after Queen Isabelle, because she was their little queen amongst all the boys.

She wondered if she'd failed her only daughter, so much so that she left and wouldn't return.

Olina thought back to the days when her children were small. Bella played with dolls and wanted to be the wife or mother when she played house with other children, yet she was like the boys in almost every other way. Never shy or quiet as some girls in school, but she held her own against any child on the school playground. No, she didn't need her brothers to protect her. So, was this just who she was? Did this independence have to do with nature, or nurture? She shook her head. It was her competitiveness to do what others could do that made her step out like this.

And if she had the chance to raise Bella again, would she have raised her any differently? No, she finally thought, because except for being competitive, she was perfect as she was. A fine woman, with a good heart. She had to believe that God would use her strengths for His good.

Her hand moved along the bottom of the photographs and stopped at Bella's picture, then put her hands to her face and cried, once again fearing for the life of her beautiful child.

ISABELLA CLEARED the stagecoach and moved as fast as her crutch would take her. Without turning around, she entered a nearby saloon looking for help. After a quick survey, she walked to the largest man leaning against the bar.

"Excuse me, sir."

His eyes widened when he saw her, and a smile crossed his face. He tipped his hat in greeting, then held it in his hand.

"I was wondering if I might be able to pay you to be my escort to the Hestand's home."

One eyebrow raised in question, so she immediately added, "It's not safe for a woman to travel alone, sir. Can you help me?"

"Certainly."

Isabella let out a breath of relief and gave him her sweetest smile. "My name is Isabella Moore."

"My name is Woodrow Miller."

"How do you do? Do you happen to know where the Hestand's live?"

His eyebrows scrunched together. "No."

"Well, then do you happen to know where the new school is?"

"Yes, that I do know. It's not too far, even with a crutch." He put his arm out for her and she grasped it like a lifesaver.

Once they set out, Isabella looked behind her. Kirkwood and Terrence were indeed following her. She could feel a firm muscle on Woodrow's arm, which largely comforted her. Too bad for them, she thought, and smiled at Woodrow as he talked about his wife and little daughter."

Around the bend, no one was about but the four of them.

"I think those men are following us," she whispered to Woodrow.

He stopped and turned. The men were about thirty feet from them and stopped as well.

"Can I help you?" asked Woodrow.

"Huh? Oh yes, we need to talk to Miss Moore."

She couldn't believe Kirkwood's boldness.

Isabella tried to pull Woodrow along, but being a big man, she couldn't budge him.

"I don't want to talk to them," she told him in a quiet voice. "They made lewd comments to me on the stagecoach. That's why I hired you to get me to the school safely."

Woodrow looked back at the men in time for him to hear, "Miss Moore is actually Mrs. Moore and I am Mr. Moore, her husband. She ran away from home and I am trying to bring her back," said Kirkwood, hat to chest.

She stomped her free foot. "That is a lie! They want me to run a whorehouse for them."

"Now come on, Isabella. It's me, your dear husband, and I want you back."

Woodrow shook his head. "I will not get involved in a family feud, Miss … I mean Mrs. Moore."

A lot of good his muscle did him, she thought. Apparently, he had a lot of muscle in his frontal lobe as well. To steady herself, she grabbed Woodrow's suit with a hand and bent over to pick up a rock.

Kirkwood and Terrence were gaining on them, so she threw a couple of pebbles at them.

They stopped to chuckle at her antics, and since they were off guard, she chucked a rock at Kirkwood's frontal lobe and down he went.

While Terrence looked on with disbelief, she hit him with another. It hit his nose, and blood spewed everywhere.

Isabella started to pick up another rock, but Terrence put up a hand and started crying. Just like her brother Caleb did the last time she'd given him a bloody nose without a rock.

Thankfully, Terrence turned away. His crocodile tears told her he'd had enough.

"You are fired from your position, Woodrow. Why don't you go help the men instead?"

Isabella could see her way to the school, and she moved toward it, feeling much calmer now.

"Okay, so I had an escort, Gabriel. It really helped a lot," she spoke aloud.

THE TOWN of Haines lay in a valley, with the Eagle Cap Mountains to the east and the Elkhorn mountains to the west. The valley contained good land for running cattle, potatoes and wheat.

A room upstairs in the home of Mr. David Hestand and

his wife Ruth was where she'd reside for the next two months. The room was comfortable enough with a full-size bed and enough books to entertain her in the evenings; however, she struggled up and down the stairs each day as her leg was still healing. Yet, this would not be forever, she knew.

Mr. Hestand worked at the town's newspaper, which was a good fit for him because he liked to read and write. As a matter of fact, he retreated into the newspaper or a book most of the time, except when she joined them for dinner.

"May I help you get dinner on the table?" Isabella asked.

"No, no. You are probably very tired after working today."

"No, I'm okay. Certainly, I can help with something."

Ruth shook her head. "I don't know how you do it. If I had to work, I'd be so tired I wouldn't be able to do a thing in the evenings."

Isabella detected a little holier-than-though attitude in the tone of her voice but wasn't sure. "I think once a person gets used to working, their bodies adjust to the schedule. People can do a lot if they put their mind to it."

"Well, I'm not going to find out. My place is in the home, not out doing a man's job."

Isabella wanted to say, "Why let the men have all the fun?" but thought better of it, because Ruth was her landlady. Instead, she said, "I don't have a husband to tend to, so I'm glad for the opportunity to teach the town's children."

"Perhaps you'll find a husband one day," Ruth said with a smile. "Until then, you have a respectable job to tide you over."

Isabella smiled in return, only because she'd looked across the table at David who was only present physically, his bespeckled eyes scanning a book she hadn't seen him bring to the table. Isabella believed her life of teaching was far more entertaining than Ruth's.

"Put the book down," said Ruth, and David came to the present, as if waking up where he sat.

BEING a teacher meant being under the close scrutiny of the town. If they'd scrutinized her during the last month, they would have never let her teach their children. Somehow, she thought, that was unfair.

Here she had to be prim and proper, she couldn't throw any rocks, even though a few times she wanted to. An escort was required anytime she left to go anywhere but the schoolhouse. She was in prison here as much as she was in her hometown with worrisome brothers.

How could Marie, she wondered, have thought things would be different anywhere else in the states? Even though the idea was hard to take, she figured she'd always have to be watched as though so frail she'd break into a million pieces at any moment.

"HOW DO you know that's true, Miss Moore?" asked Henry.

The boy asked more questions than anyone she'd ever met. She'd had a whole month of teaching and she knew where this discussion was going. "Because George Washington wrote often about what was happening in his life. That means there are records that give us this information."

"What do you mean, records?" he returned.

With an inward sigh she said, "Can someone else explain to Henry what recording something means?"

The students all looked at each other, afraid they'd be called on, except for Francine.

"Francine, can you help me please?" Her goal for Francine related to overcoming shyness.

As if condemned, she slowly stood and told Henry pretty much what she'd just said. Henry nodded.

Isabella noticed a gash, with a red circle around it, on her arm.

When school was out, she called Francine to her desk. "What happened to your arm?"

"I ran into our new barbwire fence and it cut me."

"It looks sore."

Francine glanced at it. "It'll be okay."

"I want to walk you home and talk to your father."

She stiffened and her eyes opened wide. "I'm not in trouble am I?"

"No, not at all. I'd like to meet your father."

"Okay," she said with a smile.

CHAPTER 19

Now that her leg no longer pained her, Isabella enjoyed getting out for a walk. She only hoped Francine could serve as her escort.

Isabella knew that Francine didn't have a mother, lost her to pneumonia a few years back. She couldn't imagine what that would be like.

"How do you do, Mr. Foster?" He walked to them from the barn. He was a handsome man with sandy hair and blue eyes.

"I'm just fine, Miss Moore," he said and shook her hand. "Is something wrong?"

She shook her head. "First I'd like to say that Francine is an excellent student, but I'd like her to speak up more."

"She's been shy since her mother died, I'm afraid." Francine looked down at her feet.

Isabella didn't want her to feel worse than she did already. "I don't mean to criticize; I mean to tell you that I have called on her more often to help her feel more secure in her environment. She knows the answers, don't you dear? That's more than half the battle."

Francine smiled, and so did her father. She knew that her father was proud of his only daughter.

"Would you like to come in?" he asked, fidgeting with his hat.

"Thank you, but no." She knew the townsfolk would not go for her carousing around with a widower. "I need to go, but I want to tell you something about Francine's arm."

She could see lines of concern on Mr. Foster's forehead. Francine held her arm for him to see.

"I'm thinking that her arm might be infected or heading that way. I worked with a doctor just before I came to Haines and he believed that pouring alcohol on a wound would help kill the bacteria. Anyway, I know it's none of my business, but I just thought I'd share what I know."

He rubbed his chin. "I can get a hold of some liquor."

"I know vodka works." She looked down at Francine. "It may sting a little, but it will help you heal. Then put a bandage on it for a while."

Francine nodded and Isabella turned to go.

"Miss Moore?"

"Yes, Mr. Foster?"

"My name is Mark."

"Yes, Mark?"

He smiled. "Perhaps I can call on you one day? Uh, to talk to you about Francine."

"Oh, of course," she said, with a smile. "Bring a chaperone with you. I don't want to lose my job." Perhaps her words were forward, but it was her reality.

"Certainly."

As she headed back to the Hestand's home, she walked briskly, turning her head from time to time, until she made it as far as the schoolhouse.

When had she become so fearful? she wondered. Not very

long ago she wouldn't have cared whether her actions were acceptable or not.

Suddenly she stopped in her tracks, realizing Gabriel was responsible for her new behavior. Even though she'd had a few dangerous encounters on the way to Haines, she didn't fear man as much as she feared Gabriel's disappointment in her. Whether she wanted him to or not, he indelibly left his mark on her.

She looked up at the mountains knowing Gabriel was on the other side.

She'd done her best to push him from her mind but acting out subconsciously was a different matter altogether. Wasn't her visit to Francine's father, to help sanitize her wound, proof of it as well?

In her room, she sat at her desk, going over the next week's curriculum. She had challenges teaching many levels at one time due to the range of ages amongst her students. Also, she had three who spoke a different language at home. Thankfully, the oldest of the three helped her translate to them, and most days that worked well.

Finally, her mind settled on a student who'd been absent, and she wondered if he was sick. If so, she wondered if she'd read about his illness in one of Gabriel's periodicals.

"Olina, we have a letter about Bella!"

She turned toward John, afraid to be too hopeful in case the news was not good. John smiled, and hope rose in her heart.

"Dr. Stone, found us by addressing the envelope with only my name and the city and the letter made it to us."

Olina clapped her hands together. "What does it say? What does it say?"

"Bella was in a stagecoach accident - "

"No!" Her heart plummeted.

"Wait, it says she made it through all right. She had a broken leg but it's healing properly. Bella did take a teaching job, as she'd planned, and had left for Haines when the doctor wrote this."

She put a hand on John's arm. "We can find her now." After a moment she asked, "Why didn't she tell us? Why did she let us worry?"

"The letter doesn't say, but if I know my daughter, it's because she believed we'd come get her."

"Will we, John?"

"The doctor said she planned to write us when she made it to Haines. We'll pray and wait a little longer, hope for her letter, then we go."

THE NEXT TIME Isabella saw Mark was at a church potluck, under a tree in the schoolyard. The Indian summer weather allowed an afternoon of sunshine among trees with leaves beginning to turn the colors of fall.

The men set up tables and the women loaded them with fried chicken, potatoes, corn on the cob, beans, and other vegetable dishes pulled from their gardens. Dessert consisted of cakes, pies, biscuits and jam.

As the town's schoolteacher, Isabella was granted a place at the front of the line. Afterwards, she sat down to eat on the edge of a blanket spread on the ground. When she took a bite of chicken, she remembered the turkey she'd had with Gabriel.

It seemed like ages since she'd seen Gabriel and she missed everything about him. She wondered what he was doing, how he felt about himself, now that she was not underfoot. Did he feel relief that she was no longer a burden to him? She hoped he didn't feel that way, that he'd at least cherished their talks about medicine, if nothing else. In her opinion, he had to go back to full time medicine.

Francine dropped down beside her, followed by her father. She looked over at Mark as he picked up a drumstick and started eating.

He was the opposite of Gabriel in coloring, with freckled skin and blonde hair, but quite handsome, nonetheless. Yet, she found herself in the same position she was in before she'd left Prairie City, not interested in more than friendship with the men of the town.

Mark lowered his drumstick and his smile widened as he caught her staring at him. She would not flirt, she decided, or keep him guessing the way she did the men back home.

"Nice weather we're having," she said.

"For now. Wait until you see the snow in the winter. It's pretty though."

"I will be leaving as soon as the term is up."

With a frown, he said, "I thought maybe you'd stay here, since you've made friends with the town's people."

"I appreciate the job they've given me and their friendship. It has to do with my family; I want to return to them."

"How's the land for farming over there?" She could see hope reach his eyes, making him smile again.

"My parents do all right, but they have lots of help from my brothers."

Isabella watched Francine look out at two boys, one throwing a ball as high as he could and then catch it. She laid her plate down and went to join them.

"Listen, I don't want to lead you on, and I definitely don't want to uproot your life. Friendship is all I want with you, and I am sorry to be so blunt, but I think it's best.

"I understand," he said, but frowned. He ate quietly, then left to go toss the ball with the children.

Along the street, Mrs. Porter and Mrs. Elsworth looked toward her, walking slowly and cupping their hands at their mouths so their words would be secret. She knew what they hoped, that the two of them could be one family. She was sorry to disappoint everyone, but it couldn't be helped. She missed her family and wanted to see Gabriel at least one more time.

Mark, an honorable man, came back to the blanket and they talked mostly about Francine and how she was doing in school, and what she'd be doing next.

At the end of the day, she sat on her bed and penned a letter to her family, to ask for someone from home to come and get her. A letter that she didn't think she'd ever write at the beginning of her journey, but now seemed quite appropriate.

GABRIEL WAS THINKING that he hadn't heard back from Bella's parents, so he wondered if the letter had even reached them. Most of all he thought about Bella. He'd missed her terribly but was thankful to be busy with patients and at the blacksmith shop. Soon many of the miners would leave town for the winter and he'd have less and less to do. One thing he knew for sure, being alone didn't fare well for him this winter, with only his thoughts, memories, books and medical periodicals.

CHAPTER 20

A roar of multiple hoof beats filled the air and store owners and patrons alike stepped outside to see what was happening. Six disheveled men rode into Haines, with one extra horse. The men came to an abrupt stop and tied their horses at the first saloon.

The boardwalks emptied as if the town's people expected trouble. One by one the men stepped in and filled the whole length of the bar.

"We're looking for someone," called the last man.

"I see you are all business. Would you like something to drink?" asked the bartender.

"No. We have a mission," said the oldest of the crew. After a moment he added, "We're looking for a tough character."

"You'll have to tell me who you mean, sir," the bartender replied, and the men exchanged glances and smiled.

"We're looking for Isabella Moore. Can you tell us where to find her?"

At that moment a man swung out of the bar and ran down the street.

~

ISABELLA HEARD fierce pounding at the Hestand's door, and she put a hand to her heart as Ruth answered the door. Isabella recognized the man, his name was Josh. He tried to catch his breath. "There's some men in town after Miss Moore!"

Isabella's heart started to beat as she pictured Terrence and Kirkwood in her mind's eye. She started backing to the stairwell, when she heard, "There are six of them. They all look like they're under thirty, dusty and desperate to find her."

Tenderness touched her heart and she smiled from ear-to-ear. She figured at least one of her brothers would come get her, but all six?

Instantly, she ran out past Ruth and into the street, with Josh calling after her.

"It's okay!" she shouted back. "My brothers!"

She let out a joyful cry when she saw them ride toward her. This was not the first time she noticed how commanding the team looked together. They appeared frightful until white teeth flashed against their dusty faces.

"Step back or you'll get stepped on," said Matthew, the oldest.

Just to show him, she went and hugged her horse.

In mere moments they assembled into a line, as if waiting for their queen to approach them all. One by one she hugged them and after each, she dusted herself off.

Her heart burst with love for them, and she felt that same love in return.

"Will you be visiting long?" she asked tongue-in-cheek.

The quietness was deafening.

"You're coming back home even if we have to tie you up and gag you," said Elijah, the youngest.

"Like to see you try," she said, with hands on hips.

"I think we should gag her anyway," said Matthew.

In spite of herself, she smiled in return.

"I ordered some food at the bar. How soon can you be ready

to leave?"

"My bag's been packed hoping I'd see one of you at any

time."

She didn't bring much, and she didn't leave with much. When her belongings were loaded, Elijah grabbed her handbag.

"What you got in here? Rocks?" When she pretended to ignore him, he added, "I'm not riding in front of Bella on the way back."

After saying good-bye to the Hestands', they rode past the schoolhouse. Tears formed in her eyes as she thought about the students she'd learned to care so much about. Besides this, she never really thought of this place as home, after all she'd only taught here for the two months required. Still, she learned more about who she was and what she could do. Her self-esteem had strengthened in this town of Haines.

The six men and one woman made it to the top of the highest peak and headed toward Cracker City. Isabella was glad her horse followed the one in front of her, because her mind was full of what and who lay below them in Cracker City. She'd never forgive herself if she didn't stop and see Gabriel one more time.

As soon as the trail allowed, she rode to her oldest brother. "Matthew, I want to stop in Cracker City for a few minutes."

He shook his head. "That's not the best place for a woman to be."

"For goodness sake, I'm with six big men, how can I not be safe?"

"When you passed through here before, didn't you learn that a mining town has some of the roughest characters in the West?"

She could take his words and make them fit her need. Put the blame on him, for not stopping in Cracker City. It wouldn't be her fault she'd never see Gabriel again, but his. She could move on with her life as she'd begun to shape it. Yet, could she live with that? Probably not, her heart told her.

She knew it was very hard to win an argument with this man, so she lowered her voice to nearly a whisper. "I would like to stop and thank the doctor for helping me out, so that he could know that I am safely on my way home."

"He'd probably say you weren't safe in Cracker City."

Feeling she may lose this battle, she looked down at her hands, now deeply saddened. Not seeing Gabriel ever again nearly took her breath away.

Matthew frowned. "What's with that look? Wait a minute, how old is this doctor?"

She looked up. "Around Joseph's age."

For a moment he looked relieved and then asked, "How old are you now?"

"Twenty-one."

His eyes widened and his stubble covered cheeks turned pink. "Did he touch you?"

His words were loud and firm and her eyes closed a moment in shock. Her brothers appeared to have heard him because they moved into a circle around them.

"Who would you be talking about?" said Joseph, her next eldest brother, anger in his eyes.

"The good doctor who tended our dear sister. Our only sister."

In a moment of insanity, Isabella saw a way of making Gabriel hers forever, but could see Gabriel's troubled face in her mind's eye. He didn't deserve to be saddled with her for only trying to be a good doctor. If anything, she was the one to act inappropriately, and he warned her of this. To force a man into marriage was asking for a life of emotional upheaval in her opinion.

"He did nothing I didn't want him to do."

"What?" they all said in unison and moved as close as they could get to her.

"No wonder I wanted to get away from you!"

She could tell her words twisted something in them, and she didn't want to bring up any unfounded guilt they may feel for her wanting to leave. Still, in sibling competition she didn't mention this. Yet.

"Gabriel, the doctor, treated me with more respect than you have all added into one. He did all he could to keep me from the men of the town, and did a great job doctoring my leg."

She could tell by their faces that she'd started to convince them. "I think it would be appropriate if we stopped by to see him for a moment, so that you can thank him for saving your sister from death or ruin."

There, she was finally remembering how to deal with them.

"Okay," said Luke. "Let's go."

Her heart sang with joy. Even though the commute through the mountains was cold, she could see new beauty in everything. Snowflakes dropped occasionally adding to her bliss. She was going to see Gabriel again, what better thing in life could she ever want? But her happiness simmered down to soberness as she debated what to say to him, and in front of her six brothers.

First on her list, she wanted to know about other injuries. Did he see some improvement by using vodka on wounds? Did he find out where to get carbolic acid? If he'd seen good results wouldn't he want to continue being a doctor?

Last and most important she wanted to know if he'd found some sort of peace within to help him move on. Truly, it didn't matter what he chose to do with his life as long as he made peace with God.

Everything within her wanted to move her horse to a gallop down Main Street and over the terrace to Gabriel's cabin, but she knew that kind of behavior would cause her brothers to suspect something more between them. She sighed.

Snowflakes came down more urgently now, and she knew they should be heading away from the mountains and to the valley. After that they had one more mountainous pass to tread before making it home to Prairie City. Still, if she had to crawl home through the snow on her hands and knees, she'd do it to get a chance to see Gabriel again. Angel Gabriel, she thought as they headed to his door.

Charlie came out the door and she slid down off her horse to greet him.

"How are you doing?" she asked before she gave him a bear hug.

"Standing well on two feet thanks to you and the good doc."

"I'm so glad to hear that, so glad," she said smiling immensely to show how pleased she was.

"Where's Gabriel?" she asked, when he didn't come to the door. Then she looked around and didn't see either mule.

"He's not here. Hey, I must tell you that Gabriel had some success using the alcohol on wounds. Says he's a believer now that he's seen it work for himself."

"Oh, I can't wait to talk to him about it." She looked back at her brothers who'd jumped off their horses and were moving around. "These are my brothers, escorting me home. Matthew, Joseph, Luke, Caleb, Isaiah, Elijah," she said quickly, by rote.

Charlie nodded at them. Isabella took his shoulders to move his thoughts back to her. "Where did he go? Is he at the blacksmith shop?"

He gave her a sad look, as if he felt sorry for her, and she immediately put up a guard to protect herself from hard news.

"I bought the cabin from him, so I'd have a place to winter. As you probably noticed traveling through Cracker City, many have left until the place thaws out."

"And Gabriel?"

"He told me he was going home."

Never had she had such a weight on her heart as at this moment. Home was in Illinois. "Oh, I see," she said in a breath.

"Really, you didn't miss him by many days. He would have liked to have seen you again, I'm sure, and to see that you are safe. He'd been worried about that."

As if on cue, snowflakes filled the air. "We must go. I'm very happy you are doing well. Take care, Charlie. If you are ever in Prairie City look for me.

"I will, I will."

Matthew prepared to lift her onto her horse but stopped to lift her chin. A tear had drifted down her cheek. "I'm sorry you missed him."

"Thank you," she said, but couldn't help her tears. Her brothers all looked sullen, as they moved out of Cracker City.

Some miles down the trail, she realized she'd been selfish. She learned what she wanted to learn about Gabriel from Charlie. Gabriel grew enough within to go back home. He'd learned a lot about being a better doctor in this place, and no doubt he'd be one from this point on.

Focusing on something other than herself, she looked at each brother in turn. They all looked so much older, even her younger brother had become a man. How they must love her since they'd all come for her.

Matthew's head moved back and forth always on the lookout for trouble. He'd always felt responsible for them all, she saw now.

By the time she'd left Prairie City to find a new life for herself, she was mad at her brothers. No, perhaps envious. They had so many choices, could be anything they wanted. Why did she have to be mother's helper? Maybe she'd like to take turns with the boys and tend to the cows. She loved the outdoors and would have enjoyed leading the cows to a new field, or to water.

They all had a gun strapped around their waist. She smiled thinking about the gun under her skirt that they knew nothing about. Only Gabriel knew about that. She sighed.

There was nothing she could do now. At the time she left Cracker City to go to Haines, she only knew that she had to go to her job, something she'd dreamed about for so long. It was just that she thought Gabriel would still be in Cracker City, when she needed him, she supposed. She'd been so wrong.

Sure enough, she found teaching for two months enjoyable, but found herself more enthused with student illness or illness in the neighborhood. She had wished for Gabriel's medical books so that she could study the cause and treatment.

One of the best things she'd done in life so far was being part of the treatment to help Charlie keep his leg. She'd helped prevent infection.

Suddenly Isabella realized she'd been living a lie for the last few years. Her longing for independence coupled with Marie's hopes to move toward equality for both men and women fueled her into a journey she shouldn't have taken.

She wasn't sure if she was naïve, foolish, or hardheaded. Most likely, she was all three, especially believing her family wanted to keep her from achieving her goals. There was more to life than her own personal freedoms, how shallow she'd been.

Now, she couldn't wait to see her parents, to tell them what had happened to her, what she'd learned, and most of all to apologize.

CHAPTER 21

Gabriel spent his last day as a blacksmith making surgical tools. He decided that was the most important thing he'd done as a blacksmith and a fitting end to the career.

As he made his way home, he looked to the sky and thanked God for Isabella who'd come into his life, asked questions he'd never thought of to make him think. And point him back to God.

There was nothing he could do about the war. He couldn't stop it or fix it, and because of who he was, he grieved for a long time over something he couldn't prevent.

No matter what, Gabriel found that he was fascinated with the body, it's cuts and scars, and ailments. Certainly, he wanted to stop this fascination, to move on to something else but he was never able to do this. Doctoring was a part of him, and he knew now, a gift from God.

He was and forever would be just a man who did only what he could do for others and the rest was not in his hands, but in God's. There was nothing he could do to change this, only to have faith that God would take over and do the best thing for the moment, for the time being and for all times.

Since they'd started home mid-day, Matthew selected a campsite near water in a cluster of pines. "Let's get these horses taken care of first. Come on everybody."

Isabella found she could hardly stand, weary from the trip and drained from not being able to see Gabriel again. No way could she lift a saddle right now. "I'll leave the horses to you men, and I'll put something together to eat."

In unison, every one of them turned around to look at her. "What?" she asked with hands up.

"You don't usually want to do anything that can be interpreted as woman's work, is all," said Luke.

She waved a hand in dismissal, and they frowned. "We'll be watching," said Caleb, his finger pointed her way.

"Since you don't have anything better to do than watch me breathe, why don't you go get the huckleberries we saw down the way?"

"Yes, ma'am," said one of them and they all laughed.

Isabella grumbled until she found some of her mother's bread and jerky, and a can of beans. The huckleberries made a nice addition. She hurried to set the food out before dark settled in.

Afterwards, she plopped herself against the trunk of a pine tree and remembered the last time she'd done such a thing. She wondered now how she could have sat in the woods alone with a broken leg. Anyone could have molested her in that condition, gun or no gun. She shivered at the thought.

"Bella looks cold," said Matthew. "Joseph, let's gather some blankets."

She must have been dosing because Matthew woke her when he picked her up and deposited her on blankets. Before she knew it, she was wrapped tight as a papoose. She couldn't move, she didn't want to move and was thankful that a couple of her brothers had given up blankets for her to be snug in the cold weather.

"There, that should keep her in place for the night," said Caleb.

Though she was groggy and wanted nothing more than to go to sleep, she wanted to know what Caleb was talking about. "Did you think I was going somewhere?"

"You're not going to be able to go after that doctor now," said Elijah.

Her mind flooded with memories of Gabriel. "I - "

"Did you see her bottom lip tremble?" Luke asked.

"Great, we made her cry again," said Matthew.

"No, she's asleep now and she's not going anywhere," whispered Isaiah. "I'm sleeping next to her, just in case."

"We're all sleeping next to her just in case."

Cold and travel worn, Isabella looked out at the valley, the last stretch of her trip home. Yet, not back to her old life, but to a new life, with definite plans and goals.

One of the first things she wanted to do when she got home was to sit down with Marie and tell her it's not about women gaining the upper hand at all, and it's not about breaking steadfast rules to prove something. It's about finding your God-given calling, or job is to do, and then making it work in your own special way.

Her mother always said to trust the path you're on, it'll lead you where you need to go. Her trip through the mountains was not wasted on her. The path led her to a more fitting calling, one that she can pursue safely and in her own town.

She couldn't help but smile, thinking she still wanted to compete with males. She wanted to become involved with medicine as a nurse.

"Wherever you are Gabriel, thank you for my new calling," she said softly, looking to the east, then turned back earnestly toward her new life.

OLINA MOORE STOOD on the front porch, a shawl wrapped around her thin shoulders, her auburn hair blowing in the wind. Isabella could see the moment her mother caught sight of her, even from a distance she could make out a toothy grin.

Isabella gripped the reigns and pushed her horse out in front of her brothers, to make the last leg of the trip count. Saddle weary, she slid off her horse, made an effort to stand straight and then move toward her mother.

Olina laughed and spread her arms. "My baby girl!"

"Oh, it's so good to see you!" Isabella pushed back to look at her mother. "You look thinner."

"So do you. And something else."

"Tired? Where's father?" she asked, looking around the house and out toward the barn.

"Getting some work done in the field. He couldn't just sit and wait."

Isabella nodded; she would have been the same way.

She looked back at her mother in time to see a tear fall. "It's okay, Mother. I'm here now. It's okay."

Olina nodded and wiped tears on the sleeve of her upper arm. "Come inside, dear."

A fire in the hearth filled the room with warmth. Isabella

shed her coat and boots and looked around the living area. Somehow things looked different, yet the same.

Although she'd not change anything that had happened to her for the last three months, she was glad to be back home. The knickknacks on the hearth, furniture, and pictures on the wall provided her with a cozy feeling of home. Was it only three months since she'd been gone?

Olina hugged every one of her brothers as they drifted in looking for something to eat. Thankfully, her mother had provided a nice spread of food, churned butter, cheese, bread, beef, canned applesauce and vegetables. A cake set cooling on the edge of the stove.

"The prodigal daughter has come home," quipped Caleb.

It would be funny to Isabella if it hadn't been so true. She turned to her mother to apologize but her father stepped in the house.

Isabella flew to him, kissed him, and he spun her around.

"Aw, my girl, at last."

She put her head on his chest and took a moment to enjoy feeling like a child, held by her loving father.

"Your leg doesn't look worse for wear. I'm hoping that is true."

"It's good, Father. It's good."

A brother's plate of food enticed her to join them. Her father walked her to the table.

"Stop everyone. Let's have a prayer of thanks," said John.

Heads dropped in respect and her father's words filled the room. Words of gratitude for all they were given, words asking for direction, and words of praise for the heavenly Father. And to herself she added thanks for her safety, which she now appreciated.

After supper, her brothers headed out to check on the animals and Isabella helped clean the kitchen. As Isabella had done for many years, she worked side by side with her mother preparing a smaller meal for later in the day.

"Sit down, Mother. I want to talk to you."

Her mother looked pleased, then concerned.

"It's okay. I want to apologize for the pain I've caused you and Father. I didn't leave appropriately; I didn't tell anyone I was going. I didn't let you in on my progress. It's not a very good excuse now, but I didn't think you'd let me go."

Her mother sighed, long and loud. "No, I wouldn't have let you go without an army beside you."

"I thought you were being unfair. But, I know now that you were right. I shouldn't have made the trip alone, especially through the mining district. "Yet, I've learned so much about myself and what I want to do with my future."

Her mother stiffened. "Dare I ask what it is you've learned?"

"I don't think I want to be a teacher."

"Oh?"

Her poor mother, she knew she was waiting for problematical news. "Do you still want to work?"

"Yes, and I still want to work in the world of men, but … "

Olina looked like she'd bitten into a lemon, and she couldn't let her continue to worry.

"In the field of medicine," she said trying to clarify, but only put lines into her mother's forehead. "I want to be a nurse, a very womanly thing to do since the war."

"I see. Then you're leaving again?"

"No, I am staying here. I'm going to try to worm my way into the hospital here."

Isabella didn't know her mother had stopped breathing until she gulped in some air.

"The doctor who helped me in Cracker City … I helped him with another patient while I was there. It was rewarding to help in this way."

"I am relieved, but your eyes are clouding up. What is this?"

"I miss the doctor. I didn't get to say good-bye." The tears wouldn't stop.

"But why do you cry so? Do you have feelings for him?"

Somehow her mother had brought her feelings to a head. She nodded, crossed her arms as if in pain and doubled over.

"He didn't mistreat you, did he?" Olina asked, concern in her voice.

"What?" she looked up.

"Did he try to take advantage of you?"

Any other time she would have laughed at the way her mother was trying to discuss an improper subject. "No."

"You're sure then?"

She nodded and tried to dry her eyes.

"Then I must tell you that he was here yesterday. I've been so busy welcoming you home that I forgot to tell you."

CHAPTER 22

Isabella stood up. "What?"

"He was here yesterday, looking for you."

This could not be true. He was going home. She would not get her hopes up, there had to be some mistake.

"Are you sure this was the same doctor?" she asked with her hand pulling at her mother's sleeve.

She nodded. "His name was Gabriel Stone. One of the reasons I know is because he sent us a letter telling us you were on your way to Haines. He felt we needed to know."

"He'd written to you?"

Olina nodded again.

"I guess I owe more apologies." Her heart started to beat. Gabriel had been here. "Do you know where he is? Is he just passing through? He must be just passing through."

"He didn't say. Only that he'd come by today."

Isabella flew to the door and stepped out onto the porch. She didn't see anyone coming, so she went back inside.

"I want to clean up. I need a bath."

Over and over Isabella told herself not to get excited. Just as many times, she told herself that she'd get that chance to tell him thanks for everything and to apologize for being so foolish.

Primping in the mirror took longer than it ever had, pushing her hair up, down and then up again. That was after she'd spent time drying her hair by the fire.

Still, Gabriel hadn't arrived.

"Are you sure you're okay?" her mother asked.

"Yes."

"You're wringing your hands, making me nervous too, and I don't know why."

Isabella grabbed a shawl that matched her blue dress and stepped out onto the porch. A man on a horse headed their way. No - a mule, she was certain, and started running as fast as her shoes allowed. Adrenalin shot through her and her heart pounded in her ears.

Gabriel jumped off his mule and met her halfway.

"Oh, Gabriel! I'm so glad to see you."

"I'm glad to see you, too, Bella."

"I came by to see you in Cracker City, but you'd left. For home!" She couldn't help the tears that followed.

He took her in his arms and hugged her so tight she could hardly breathe.

Isabella knew he would be leaving soon, so she had no time to spare. "I've already spent the afternoon apologizing to my family and now I want to apologize to you for being immature, stubborn, and stupid!"

"Oh, so you've realized that?" he said with a smile.

"I've missed your smile."

"You brought it back to me and then took it away again."

"But now it's back." She stepped on her toes and kissed his lips.

"We have an audience."

Isabella looked back to see every member of her family

assembling in the front of the house. "I need to tell you a few things. First of all, yes, I'm sorry for the pain I caused everyone, but I learned so much. One of the things I wanted to do was thank you for introducing me to the field of medicine. You helped me realize that teaching isn't what I want to do after all."

He lifted an eyebrow. "You want to be a doctor?"

"No. No. I want to be a nurse."

"You'll be a good one." With furrowed brow he added, "Does that mean you're leaving town again?"

"No, I've learned my lesson, I'm staying here."

"That's good."

Isabella realized she should feel desolate since he was going home without her, but she couldn't help responding to his smile. She kissed his lips again.

"Your brothers are crossing their arms, they don't look too happy."

"It's okay."

"I have a few things to say to you, too. I've done some thinking since you've been gone, mostly about the war. Your questions made me wonder why I had to experience the hell of screaming patients, cut off limbs, fight disease, and watch people die. I didn't think this was what I'd dreamed of doing for so long, but I now know it is. I'd been living the bad, not looking for the good to come from it all. And that is learning from the experience, to see what went wrong, to find out how to improve, and build upon what I'd learned in the medical field.

"So, I'm excited now because I know what I what to do. I want to continue working on preventing infection. I want to help by wearing a uniform, keep things clean, and using carbolic acid on wounds to clean them. You know, all that we've talked about."

She nodded.

"The Civil War helped doctors see what's needed and to start making change. I step up to the challenge."

"I'm so happy to hear you say that. And women did have a very important role in the Civil War. Her role as a nurturer, a caretaker, a cleaner, and organizer of her family's life, carried over into the war effort. These same things needed in a man's home were needed in a man's war. When these things were addressed, lives were saved, and limbs were spared. From this came new discoveries into medicine, changing things from that time forward. I want to be part of that."

He reached out and touched a tendril of hair that fell from her pinned up hair. "Nice thinking. Yes, I think a woman's hand should be in all things."

She nodded and smiled.

"Your family is inching closer. Like they have a wild animal cornered and they don't want to scare it away."

"Oh, dear."

"There is only one thing I can do." Gabriel got down on one knee. "I believe our paths crossed for a reason. You, Bella, have made a difference in my life. You took a grieving man and asked provoking questions that made me think. Made me want to do the right thing. Make me want to serve God, follow His plan for me. I cannot take this lightly."

"Thanks for all the nice things you're saying, but my family will get the wrong idea. Besides, you're going to get your pants dirty."

With a big smile, he said, "I love you. Marry me. *Marry* me, Bella. Say you will."

She could not get her hopes up, she could not! "But, you're leaving, you're going back to Illinois."

"No. I've come home. Home to you here. I want to work as a doctor here in Prairie City. I've made about all the tools I need as a blacksmith, and now all I really need is a nurse."

"Squee!" She hugged him and they both fell over into the

dirt, which spooked the mule and apparently her family, because she heard guns cocking around them.

After rising to their feet, Isabella turned to her family. "You have nothing to worry about. I'm not leaving town. I've been asked to work as a nurse for a doctor in town. Gabriel Stone is the finest doctor and man I've ever known. He's a God- fearing man and about to be my husband."

"Ma, you ready to have someone else worry about her for a while?" asked Matthew.

Olina and John smiled at each other.

John reached out his hand to Gabriel. "Come inside, let's eat and celebrate."

ABOUT THE BOOK

Cracker City is now called Bourne, Oregon and it is indeed six miles from Sumpter on a gravel road. I tried to make the setting as authentic as I could, but all else is a work of fiction. Some gold mining is still done to this day and there are cabins of various ages sprinkled along the Main Street.

I saw the Bourne-Haines stage route on a forest service map and have spoken with people who have driven over it with an all-terrain vehicle (ATV). The route crosses over the Blue Mountains as it does in this story.

If you enjoyed reading the book, please leave a review. It is the best way to thank an author.

ABOUT THE AUTHOR

MARY VINE is an author, publisher, speaker and retired educator. She writes contemporary and historical romantic fiction, a time travel series, and inspirational children's books. Mary, and her husband can usually be found in Southwest Idaho or Northeast Oregon.

To learn more about Mary and all her books, visit her website at: http://maryvine.com

OTHER BOOKS BY MARY VINE

CONTEMPORARY ROMANCE

Maya's Gold

A Place to Land

A Haunting in Trillium Falls

Snake River Rendezvous

HISTORICAL ROMANCE

Wanting Moore

Time Travel

Nugget of Time

Goldbrick

Summer Solstice

INSPIRATIONAL CHILDREN'S BOOKS

The Big Guy Upstairs

Biju Silver Lining

WINDTREE PRESS

Thank you for purchasing this Windtree Press publication. For other books of the heart, please visit our website at https://windtreepress.com.

Windtree Press
Portland, Oregon

www.ingramcontent.com/pod-product-compliance
Lightning Source LLC
Chambersburg PA
CBHW030620130626
46552CB00002B/652

* 9 7 8 1 9 5 0 3 8 7 3 5 9 *